Mill Girl

My Story.

Mill Girl

The Diary of
Eliza Helsted, Manchester, 1842-1843

By Sue Reid

For my sister

While the events described and some of the characters in this book may be based on actual historical events and real people, Eliza Helsted is a fictional character, created by the author, and her diary is a work of fiction.

This edition produced for the Book People Ltd,
Hall Wood Avenue, Haydock, St Helens WA11 9UL

First published in the UK by Scholastic Ltd, 2002

Text copyright © Sue Reid, 2002

ISBN 0 439 95497 5

Ancoats, Manchester, England
1842

Saturday 23 April, 1842

I didn't go to the mill today. I always go on Saturdays, come rain or shine. Father says he likes to see my cheery face. As soon as the bell goes I'm up at once grabbing for my shawl, my clogs clattering as I run down our court. Then I stand by the gate on tiptoe and watch for Father among all the people pouring out of the mill. When it's wet, the women pull their shawls tightly round their heads and the men walk quickly, heads down, jackets pulled up close round their ears. It's hard to pick out Father's face then.

It's nearly always raining in Manchester.

You can see the big dark walls of the mill from our court. The houses huddle round it in little rows, back to back. Sometimes I squeeze my eyes tight to shut out the sight of it. I try and imagine clear blue skies and green fields, like the countryside where Grandfather was born. But when I open my eyes again the mill is *still* there. I hate the mill. Mother does too. It's one of the few things we seem able to agree on. But I don't want to think about the mill now. Or Mother. Or how she looked at Emmy when she left. At those big dark eyes in that pale face, eyes so like William's. My brother. But much more than my brother he was. My best friend. Two years ago today he died.

Mother seemed so far away. In another world almost. I watched as she wrapped her shawl round her head. "I'm sorry, Eliza, I won't be long," she said, one hand already on the door. She didn't say where she was going but I knew. I didn't say anything, I just couldn't. I stood looking at the ground, trying not to cry, trying not to think about William, and she said sharply, "I should think you'd want to be looking after your little sister."

I felt so upset when she said that and as soon as she had gone I ran upstairs. I wanted to be alone. I didn't want to think about William. Didn't want to remember how Mother had looked at Emmy. But however hard I tried to push them away the memories followed, crowding into the room with me. I told myself that soon Father would be home and then I would feel comfortable again. But I felt so sad and lonely and try as I might I couldn't stop thinking about William. I wished I had someone to comfort me.

That's when I thought of this diary. I've been wondering what to do with this book ever since

Miss Croom gave it to me yesterday. She says I'm to practise my writing in it but I don't think she'll mind if I begin a diary. I can practise my writing *and* write down everything I think and feel. I'm hoping it'll be a real friend.

I sat a moment, just holding the book in my hands. It is so beautiful. I love to look at the white pages, still so clean and fresh, and feel the soft blue ribbon that binds them all together. I have never had anything this nice before. But best of all are the words Miss Croom has written in ink on the first page. I fair burst with pride when I read them.

To Eliza Helsted. For excellent progress. April 1842

Miss Croom says I'm her best pupil! She says that if I go on as I do now, perhaps she will let me help her with the little ones. I'm dying to tell Father and see the pride in his face too. Me – a teacher! No one in our family has *ever* done that. Sat there thinking about it for a while. And then I remembered that the bell had gone. All the things I was meaning to write about will have to wait, for Father will be home soon and I haven't even got the water for his wash!

As I write it is late and Father is home at last. We'd known he'd be late for that Bob Wavenshawe had come round to warn us. I'd heard the knock at the door and jumped up at once and thrown it open, ready to hug Father. Was I shocked when I saw Bob standing there. It still makes me feel sick now to think how I nearly toppled off the step into him! And wasn't he pleased! He gave a sort of smirk and rubbed those yellow fingers of his together. I can't bear that smile. It's as if he knows things about you, things that could get you into trouble. Even though all he said was that Father would be late, I could see that wolfish look in his eyes – as though he could say a lot more if he chose to.

Bob's Father's piecer – has been since William died. Father says he's good at his job but I think Father took him on in a bit of a hurry for everything went topsy-turvy then, and I don't think Father really knew what he was doing. Bob's old to be a piecer, Father says, nigh on 26. He doesn't think Bob will ever get to be a spinner like him. I'm sorry, for I don't want him to go on working with Father.

Mother got back soon after Bob had left. She looked as though she'd been wrung through the mangle – so drawn and tired. I told her what Bob had said and I heard her mutter something that sounded like "those Chartists". She looked so put out. Whenever Mother's cross with Father she goes on about the Chartists. I must tell you – Mother hates the Chartists, and whenever I ask her why, she says that they're people who'll help Father lose his job and she'd rather he'd spent more time with the union and less with that Irish rabble. It's at times like this that I miss William most. He always found time to explain things I don't understand.

Grandfather called me over then and asked me to rub some ointment on his hands. He'd been sitting there so quiet I'd not noticed he'd got back from Mrs Legg's. As I took his hands in mine he told me in a whisper not to mind Mother – she was just upset. I almost managed a smile. Poor Grandfather! He suffers from rheumatism but swears that Mrs Legg's ointment soothes him greatly.

Emmy and I had just finished laying the table ready for supper when Father came in. I rushed up to him and he picked me up and hugged me. His head and jacket were covered in cotton fluff from the mill and a bit caught in my throat and made me cough. But I didn't mind – I was *so* happy to see him. I whispered against his jacket what Miss Croom had said. "My clever clever lass," he murmured, hugging me again. He sounded so proud! But it was strange – when I looked up into his face it wasn't smiling at all and his eyes were all bright – as though my words had made him sad and I couldn't think why they'd do that. That was when I felt the old fear return. Nearly every Saturday now I feel like this, full of dread, wondering if Father will come home and say that he's been turned out. So many mills are closing, and so many spinners are losing their jobs. I don't know what we would do if Father lost his.

Mother was standing, arms akimbo. "Well?" I heard her say tartly. Father put me down and then, ever so slowly, put his hand into his pocket. "Well now, bonny lass," he said, so seriously that I felt my breath catch for a minute. I watched as he held out his hand to Mother. Something glinted and chinked in his palm – something hard and bright and shining – and I found I could breathe again. Mother didn't look too happy, mind, as she counted out the coins – and she put the money slowly into the pot on the mantel where we keep Father's wages.

We sat to our meal of bacon and potatoes then and I tried hard not to look at the empty place across the table from me where William used to sit. But when I looked up I saw that Mother's eyes were on it too. And as I think about that now, I feel like crying all over again.

Sunday 24 April

Something woke me early this morning. Got out of bed to listen, but my footsteps creaked loudly on the boards and I heard a sudden "shush" and a silence and then this low rumble started up again from the next room. I couldn't hear a thing after that, even though the wall is paper-thin. Upstairs is really only one room – Father put up a sort of partition to make it two when we came to live here. One for him and Mother, and the other for Emmy and me. Grandfather sleeps downstairs on the settle. He says he doesn't mind that it's hard.

Think I must have fallen asleep again then for when I got up and went downstairs Father had gone out and Mother's eyelids were red. Emmy and I crept like mice round her. Felt upset. Sunday's the only day we can all be together and it's so rare that Father's at home now.

When he's not at the mill, he's out on "business". What sort of business I don't know for sure, but I think I can guess for it makes Mother so cross! And then Grandfather woke up with a start and gave one of his harrumphs – and somehow made things still worse. "There goes another one," he rumbled, looking at the empty place at table where Father should be. "There's many a man caught by the demon..." he went on. Emmy and I looked at him – all agog we were – but Mother stopped him with one of her looks. Mother's look could make even Mr Thomas, master of the mill, quake.

I went over to Grandfather and took his hand in mine, feeling the twisted fingers and dry wrinkled skin. He smiled at me and gave my fingers a squeeze and as usual I was surprised by his strength. Grandfather was a weaver when he was young but he didn't work in the mill like Father – he worked at home on the loom in his cottage. Everyone says what fine cloth Grandfather wove – so Grandfather says! I settled myself down next to him and listened as he told me about his life in the country. It's a story I've heard so many times before but I never tire of it. How he'd begun to help his father at his loom when he could barely walk. Proudly he told me about the gold watch his father wore when the family went to chapel. And about the mahogany table and finely polished clock on the mantelpiece, the cabinet full of china. Father always laughs when Grandfather says that. He says that he's forgotten what hard days those were. Where is all that fine china now? he asks.

But oh – how I wish we could live in the country. Grandfather could tell how I felt I knew because he twinkled at me and hobbled over to the dresser. Puffing a bit, he opened the bottom drawer and pulled out a book. It's not a proper book, not really – just bits of paper tied together. Full of dried flowers it is – Grandfather picked and pressed them years ago from the fields near the cottage where he lived with Grandmother. As he opened the book I settled down beside him again and Emmy came close too and leaned over my shoulder. Even Mother put down her work for a moment and came over, a softer look in her eyes. There's something still of the country in our family. We're not town people, not really.

Monday 25 April

School today. Usually I'm so pleased to be there but as we were walking there this morning, me half pulling Emmy along behind me as usual, I realized that Mother had forgotten our pennies. Not the first time either, mind! I felt so embarrassed that I'd come empty-handed yet again that I slunk in behind Emmy and went to sit on the half-empty back bench, the place I used to sit when funny old Miss Pedlar taught us. I kept my head down and did not speak in class all morning.

As soon as lessons were over, I rushed over to Emmy's bench and hoicked her out. It's a long time since I've left school so quick. After, I helped Mother with the washing and then she sent me down to Mr Owen's for a ha'p'orth of tea and sugar, telling me to tell him that she'd settle next Saturday. I don't know what's wrong with her just now – she's so jumpy and cross. I was glad to get out of the house. And I love going down to Mr Owen's. You have to walk right down Great Ancoats Street to get there. It's a bit of a walk but I don't mind. I like it, at least in the evening when it's so busy and bustly; there's that horsy smell about it – you notice it long before you see the horses, very strong it is, but I'd far rather it than the smell down our court just now. And once you're there you have to keep your eyes sharp about you as the wagoners and cabbies never seem to see you. Then, when the mill bell goes, the lights come on in the gin palaces and beerhouses and you have to skirt round them too.

But what I like best is watching the little shops as they open up for the evening. All sorts there are – butchers and bootmakers, drapers and tobacconists, sweet-sellers, tailors, pawnbrokers and big rag-and-bone warehouses. Some putting up shutters, others locking doors for the night. Then behind – every 20 to 30 yards – the great black cotton mills and warehouses. Out of the corner of my eye I can see the light shining out of the hundreds of little windows like little blinking eyes watching you, all six storeys of them, but many mills looking even taller, the slender chimneys so high they seem to vanish into the fog. Even here you can hear the rattly din and the gushing of the steam engine, and I always long for the dark to fall properly and the engines to stop – for then the smoky air clears a little and my eyes don't feel so itchy.

But today, even though the engines were still banging away, it wasn't as noisy as usual; there weren't so many people on the streets and a lot of the shops looked as if they wouldn't be opening up at all. There were all those hawkers, mind, swarming round me like wasps, their trays of sweets and cakes shoved up under my nose – even worse than the children pulling at my skirts. But oh! The smell of that gingerbread! I wished I could buy a piece for just the sight and smell of it was making me feel so hungry.

To get to Mr Owen's, I turn off just before Great Ancoats Street reaches Oldham Road and the railway. That's where the Irish gather. Mother says they're all Chartists. They sounded so excited this evening, arms waving, eyes flashing. I'd have loved to stop and listen, but as I walked past they were so many talking at once that I couldn't make out what they were saying. One of them winked at me and I found myself smiling back. I like them.

I'd seen so many shops shut down, it made me wonder if Mr Owen's would be open or not. But as I turned into his street I saw him at the door and the shutters back. I followed him in and told him what Mother had said. Mr Owen just grunted. He gave me the tea and sugar, but he looked none too happy about it.

Walked back the long way, by the canal, watching the barges slide down the dark and scummy waters, laden with coal and bales of cotton from the mills. There were people squatting on the banks too, filling pails with the oily-looking water; I don't know how they can do that. Sometimes it's all green and frothy near the banks with the mucky waste spilling out from the dye works. Makes me shudder to see them. I'm glad our court has a tap.

I'd just got home when I heard the most peculiar sounds – a rumbling and a knocking which seemed to come from right under my feet. Even the ground seemed to be shaking with it. Then as suddenly as they had begun, the noises stopped. The Brighams' door opened and Jack Brigham came out, a bucket in his hand. His face was streaked with oil and dirt and I watched as he ran down the court to the tap. I couldn't think what he'd been doing to make himself so filthy!

Tuesday 26 April

Sat at the back of class again today. Miss Croom gave me the oddest look when she saw me there again, for that's where the mill children sit when they come in from work. Not much gets done on that bench, most of the children nod off as soon as they sit down. She didn't say anything, mind, though I saw her eyebrows go up. As soon as lessons finished, I hurried out, Emmy skipping along behind me. I know I must remind Mother to give us the money for school. But this evening I just couldn't find the courage. But I must and soon. I can't hide on that back bench for ever.

Wednesday 27 April

Back of the class again. When the lesson had finished Miss Croom came straight over to my bench and asked me what was wrong. "Are you all right, Eliza?" she said, sitting down next to me. Felt so guilty when I saw that concern on her face. "It's a long time since you sat here." I couldn't speak. I did not know what to say. I heard her sigh. "You are my best scholar, Eliza," she said. "But your work this week has been slovenly and bad. Is something troubling you?" Her words made me flinch. I sat there, silent. What could I say? I wished she'd leave me be. "I do not want to see you waste your ability," she said at last. Then quietly she reminded me that I've not brought our pennies for school. Two weeks' we owe her, she said. I was so embarrassed that I felt myself blush right up to my hair and I heard myself promising I'd bring them in the morning. Hope I'll not have to break that promise.

It is late but I must tell you though I can scarcely bear to write the words. I AM TO LEAVE SCHOOL – Emmy too. Not that Emmy minds – she doesn't care about it as I do and danced round the room when Mother told us. Father wouldn't even look at me. He just stared at the floor, twisting his cap in his hands as he told me that there's no money to spare. That it's not right to ask Miss Croom to wait any longer for it. I didn't say a word. Just went upstairs, my head held high. I could feel their eyes on me, but I didn't look back. I didn't want them to see how much I minded.

Mother came upstairs later but I turned my face away and pretended to be asleep. I heard her put a tray with oat cakes and buttermilk down by my bed. "I'm so sorry, Eliza, lass," she said softly. "But think on it. You're thirteen now. Most girls have left school and are working long before that. You surely hadn't thought you'd stay on much longer, had you?" I could hear her quiet breathing while she waited for an answer from me. I knew deep down what she said was true but I didn't care. I just wanted her to go. I lay there very still and at last I heard her tiptoe softly from the room.

Can't bear to think that I have to leave, but it's not just that that's making me feel so awful inside. Why's there so little money coming into the house, so little that even Emmy has to stop school? Father still has his work at the mill. Up and out by 5.30 each day – except Sunday. Can't think why they won't tell me what's wrong. On and on they go about how old I am and yet somehow they won't trust me. If I'm old enough to leave school and begin work, why am I not old enough to be trusted? Feel too upset to write more.

Thursday 28 April

My last day at school. I went dragging my feet. I've never walked there so slowly. Emmy pulled at my hand to hurry me. I could tell that she was longing to tell her friends that this was to be *her* last day. I've never known her so eager.

When we got there Emmy rushed straight in but I stopped awhile outside. I stared and stared at the red brick walls, blackened with smoke, just like all the other buildings in Ancoats. I felt as though a big gate was being banged shut in my face.

Lessons had already begun when I crept in at last and I slipped into my old place on the front bench. As I sat down, I noticed how few pupils there were on the benches around me. I made an angry mark on my slate and the chalk broke into pieces and rolled on the floor. I left them lying there and stared out of the window. I don't think I took in a word all morning. After lessons were over I marched up to Miss Croom, gave her the money we owed her and told her we'd not be coming back. My face went all hot and red. "Oh, Eliza," she said. "Many of my scholars have had to leave school, it's nothing to be ashamed of."

But it was to *me*! I couldn't bear to hear any more. I seized Emmy's hand and pulled her out of her seat. I didn't let go until we were out of the building, though Emmy cried that I was hurting her. I didn't look back. Not once.

Mother gave me a right scolding when she saw Emmy's face swollen from crying, and the tears I'd been holding back just burst out of me then. Why must she always take Emmy's part? Why does she never understand how *I'm* feeling? And when it comes back to me how rude I was to Miss Croom, I feel worse still. It isn't her fault that I have had to leave school, is it? Feel so ashamed.

Friday 29 April

Such a heavy feeling in my stomach when I woke this morning. I didn't hurry to get up and I pretended not to hear when Emmy called me for breakfast. At last

Mother came to the stairs and bawled for me. "The fire needs laying and there's a deal of mending you can help me with," she said. I pulled a face. If there's one thing I hate, it's sewing.

Father came home for his dinner today. He didn't stop long, mind, just spooned up a few mouthfuls of potato pie where he stood, though Mother wanted him to sit down and eat properly for he looked so weary. It turned out then that he'd only come by to warn us that there's trouble in the town. There's been an attack on a bread shop he said, and we're to be careful when we go out. I saw Mother look anxiously at Emmy. She just can't stop fretting about her. If it's raining, she might catch a chill, or if it's dry, she might pick up something even worse from the bad vapours in our court. Now she has the dangers stalking the Ancoats streets to add to her list of fears. But Emmy's a strong and healthy child. It's rare for her to suffer a day's illness – she's not frail like our William was.

Saturday 30 April

Saturday again – our big cleaning day. Not just in our house – on Saturday the whole court sets to with scrubbing brushes. As soon as the breakfast plates have been cleared away, all the doors open wide and we run down to the tap at the end of our court, buckets swinging between us. Sometimes there's a sort of race to see who can get to the tap first. But not on the way back, mind – we try to be more careful then for Mother says water's precious and we daren't spill it, not a drop. Then Mother and I set to with cloths and brushes, scrubbing down every surface until our arms ache. The greyish walls, the dusty floor – everything must get a thorough wipe down. Even the furniture is scrubbed, for the sooty smoke from the mill gets into the house and dirt settles everywhere.

After we've finished we wash and then we make plans for Sunday when Father's home. Mother's been talking about taking us to Green Heys Fields one day soon. Not a word was said about it today, mind. If it hadn't been for Emmy's whining I don't think a word would have been said in our house all morning! Mother went about the chores, lips set tight like a trap. But whatever's on her mind she's keeping it close to her chest.

By the time the mill bell had started to clang, I'd had enough of it and I wanted to get out. I didn't want to see Father either, mind, so I didn't go down to the mill. Just upstairs to our room. There's really nowhere else to go in our little house unless you count the cellar where we store the coal. Anyway, it was as well I didn't bother for he was late home again. Mother gave him such a scolding when he finally got back, for his tea was cold on the table, but I don't think he even heard her. He was in such a peculiar mood. Restless, not able to stand still. Pacing up and down. Such an odd look in his eyes too – I can't explain it properly but it was as though he was excited about something. Our living room is very small and it's a bit of a squash when we're all at home, but I don't think he saw *any* of us. And now, as I sit writing, I realize that it's only a week since I began this diary. Just one week! I cannot believe how much my life has changed since then...

Sunday 1 May

Mrs Brigham tapped on our window early this morning. She had that big basket of hers over one arm and little Michael was jumping about at the end of the other. Michael's big brother, Jack, was with them too. For a moment his brown eyes caught mine and I noticed how his face changed when he smiled. Like William's did. Strange – I'd not noticed that before. Jack's the same age as William and he works at the mill as his father's piecer. He and William were such friends – almost as close as we were I think. Always in and out of each other's houses. But we don't see much of Jack now – haven't done since William died.

Mrs Brigham and Mother were having one of those strange conversations of theirs through the window. Mrs Brigham and Mother are great friends and they often "talk" like this. They picked up the habit when they worked in the weaving shed. It's so noisy in there you can only make yourself understood by making signs with your hands and pulling silly faces. Mee-mawing they call it. Sometimes it looks so funny that I want to laugh. After a minute or two of this Mrs Brigham waved goodbye and we watched them go, Michael hopping and skipping and pulling on his mother's arm to hurry her. I just knew they were going to Green Heys Fields. I didn't see why we couldn't go too. Sometimes Mother's so unfair!

We knew the Brighams were back when those strange noises I'd heard last week began again. Such a hammering and banging that our little house seemed to shake with it. Even Mother heard it. Anyway, after about a half-hour of this, Mother had had enough, and I was sent round to see what they were about.

"It's just Jack playing with his inventions," laughed Mrs Brigham. "I'll be glad if you can get him to stop." We went together to the top of the cellar steps and I peered down into the dark. At first I couldn't see anything at all and then I saw Jack's eyes bright in the dark, his face all smeary with oil and his hands dirty. He grinned up at me and asked if I wanted to see what he was doing. I felt a little shy but I took the candle Mrs Brigham gave me and made my way down, taking care not to slip on the greasy steps.

That invention of Jack's is the oddest-looking thing! It's supposed to make the spinning mule safer for the little scavengers who crawl underneath, but I couldn't have told that from looking at it. Looked just like a heap of old scrap to me! I tried telling Jack that he was very clever but I think my face must have showed what I *really* thought because he suddenly said gruffly that he wouldn't expect a girl to understand. Well, when he said that I thought I'd burst I felt that annoyed! I told him that I was just as bright as him, even if I'd had to leave school and spend my time cooking and cleaning. He looked at me for a minute.

"Most girls have to work," he said bluntly. "You're *lucky* to learn how to keep house!" How *dare* Jack Brigham talk to me like that! I am as capable as him and one day he will find that out. Feel too cross to write more.

Monday 2 May

Mother went out early this morning without a word – just left me with this great pile of washing. My heart sank when I saw it. Next to sewing and rough-stoning the floor it's the job I hate most. Emmy, of course, had skipped out to join the other children in the court as soon as the door had shut behind Mother so I had to do all the work. I scrubbed until my hands felt raw with it, and put the washing through the mangle. Then I called Emmy in and together we hung it out to dry across the court. The wind was brisk and it caught the washing and blew it back into our faces, making Emmy laugh. I was glad of it, though, for it will blow away the smoke and the mill soot will not dirty our drying clothes. Sometimes when I bring the washing in it's grey and we have to begin all over again.

This afternoon Mother went down to the mill with Father's tea as usual. Before William died, I'd sometimes go. I hated going into that spinning room, and Father never stopped when I went in – just took his tea from me with a nod and maybe a smile. He doesn't like his wheels to be stopped more than need be, for spinners are paid by the piece and the more Father spins the more he's likely to earn. I'd not linger long either – that room is so hot and airless and thick with the smell of oil. The windows are often kept tightly shut so that you can scarcely breathe in there in summer. Father says they have to be shut, so the draughts don't whistle through and break the threads faster than the piecers can mend them. And the noise – I haven't told you about that! Father says it doesn't bother him much but I don't see how it can't – all those roaring machines, the whirling spindles, rumbling shafts, squeaking wheels and straps. I can't believe it's worse in the weaving shed but Father says it is, and that's why Mother's so deaf now.

William would keep his head down too – he'd not dare take his eye off the moving lines of thread even for a moment in case one needed piecing up – but sometimes I'd get a wink from him, or from Jack Brigham over the way piecing the threads for his father. But the little scavenger – whenever I saw him, lying flat out under the machine, or huddled under snatching up the waste, one eye on the carriage so that it didn't come back too quick and catch him, I'd shudder. Michael does that job now – he's nine, a year older than Emmy. You can't work in the mill until you're nine now. Father says it's the law.

Tuesday 3 May

My life is just an endless round of chores. This is how I spent today.

Morning:

Fetched the water for washing from the tap.

Cleaned out the hearth.

Rough-stoned the floor. (I had to go into every little corner and I was not allowed to stop until I could see my face in the flags.)

Boiled potatoes in the pot for our dinner.

Afternoon:

Helped Mother patch our clothes with scraps of fustian and woollen cloth from clothes that are too worn for wear. There's no money for new.

Wednesday 4 May

Mother nearly scalded herself this evening. An explosion so loud that it rattled the windows, made us clutch each other in fright and Mother drop the bucket of water she was holding. We watched in dismay as the boiling water ran all over the floor. After we'd mopped it up we crept to the door, still clinging on to each other. I don't know what we expected to see out there. A heap of rubble perhaps! But no sooner had I opened the door than another loud bang made us all jump back inside again. And then I saw the long tail of a rocket burst into a thousand stars over my head.

Heedless of Mother's calls, I dropped the bucket and ran with Emmy to the entrance of the court where a small crowd had gathered. I stood and looked up at the fireworks exploding into the sky. I'd never seen *anything* so beautiful. Found myself wishing that I could leap up and grab the tail of a rocket and be carried high up into the sky, far far away from Manchester. I'd hold on tight and then float softly down into another world – a world where I'd look out of my window each morning on to green fields.

When we went back inside we found Mother ironing with such vigour it was a wonder she didn't set our aprons alight. "The rich may have money to burn," she said, thumping the iron up and down. "But *I* do not know how they can squander their money on fireworks when so many families have nothing to fill their stomachs."

She stopped suddenly when she saw our faces. It was the first time Mother'd said anything to us about what's happening in our town. Does she think I am blind and not able to see or think for myself? I know full well that there's trouble in Manchester. I am thirteen – no longer a child. I wish she'd remember that.

Friday 6 May

Father was home very late last night. Emmy and I had gone up to bed by the time he came in. Mother tried to hide her worry in anger. I hated to hear her mutter round the house, slamming down the plates on the table. Even Emmy felt the lash of her tongue – Emmy who can do no wrong!

This morning after the chores were done, I sat with Grandfather's book of pressed flowers in my lap. Usually it cheers me to look at them but today, hard though I tried to concentrate, my thoughts remained in the little troubled room. If only they'd tell me what's wrong. Is it to do with the Chartists? Is it because of *them* that Father came home so late last night? Are they the reason for Mother's red eyes?

Saw Jack Brigham walk past our house this evening. He glanced briefly through the window as he passed. I caught his eye but he scarcely seemed to notice me. But then I remembered – *I'm* nothing but a stupid girl to him.

Saturday 7 May

Mother's begun to teach Emmy how to patch and mend our clothes, and already she seems to be better at it than me. I felt such a pang inside as I watched them sitting close together in the window in the pale late afternoon light. Mother's that gentle with Emmy, so patient when she makes a mistake. I put a few more coals on the fire and stirred it vigorously. The flames leaped up, their shadows dancing on the whitewashed walls. Mother frowned when she saw what I was doing. "Go easy on the coal, Eliza," she said. If only she'd spare a little of that softness for me.

Sunday 8 May

Today Father told us that both Barrett's and Sharp's mills have turned out their workers.

At first I didn't know what he was on about and I couldn't understand why the room had gone so quiet. Then I remembered – Bill Armthwaite works at Barrett's mill. He's a big man, with a gruff manner and a growing brood of children. The Armthwaites have lived in our court for over two years now. When they first moved here they had three children and since then, two more have arrived. They keep themselves to themselves, but Emmy sometimes plays with the two eldest.

Mother got up and I watched as she reached for her shawl and began to fuss about. "I'll just pop round. See what I can do to help."

She told me to fetch candles, bread and milk. I couldn't help noticing how her hands trembled as she took some lumps of coal and sticks of kindling from the fireplace and added them to the food in the basket. This is the first time someone in our court has lost their job. It brought home to me just how bad things have got and I felt guilty to think how I've fussed about leaving school. At least *Father's* still got a job to go to.

Bill Armthwaite's eldest two boys work at Lever's mill. We're all praying that they don't lose their jobs too. But Dick and Tom are scavengers. Father says they earn only a pittance and that they're paid part of their wages in kind – food they must buy from the mill shop. It's a rotten system that, for the masters charge what they like, and there's nothing the poor hands can do about it. And how can you pay the rent and feed seven hungry stomachs on a few miserable shillings a week?

I wasn't surprised when bread and cheese were all that was laid out when we sat down together. Earlier, I'd helped Mother plan a hearty meal of beef and potatoes for our dinner. I'd been looking forward to it for meat's a rare treat in our house now. But I think it would have choked us to have eaten so well when the Armthwaites have so little.

When someone's in trouble, everyone pulls together. This evening I saw Mrs Legg pull herself slowly up from her cellar home. One trembling hand held a bunch of those strange-smelling plants she grows in her cellar. I watched as she hobbled over to the Armthwaites' house. Mrs Legg has little enough she can call her own. But even she has found something to give. Sometimes I feel so proud that I live in our court.

Monday 9 May

Little Michael was injured at the mill this afternoon. Mr Brigham said he forgot to duck and the machine banged into him. Too tired to see it, Mr Brigham said bitterly. His face was full of anguish and his big hands hung loosely by his sides as he stood looking down helplessly at the table where Michael was lying. He told us he'd seen him suddenly throw up his arm to protect his head, and then he'd fallen backwards under the machine. Jack and one of the other piecers dragged him clear, and then Jack and Mr B carried him back home between them. Mr Brigham said he could have been killed and that he was lucky only his arm was hurt. It's a deep cut, mind – I had to turn away and sit down quick when I saw it, my legs were swimming under me.

"Never again will a child of mine work at that place. *Never*," I heard Mother mutter darkly to herself as she put water on the Brighams' fire to heat. She spoke so quietly that I could scarcely hear her, but her words made me feel so glad. I couldn't bear to work at the mill.

Poor Mrs Brigham! Mr Brigham told her that he can't get an infirmary order until Thursday. Young Mr Thomas, the master's son, said that they have none to spare. Mrs Brigham burst out crying when he said that, for she fears that infection may set in if the doctor cannot treat the wound quickly.

Mother helped Mrs B into a chair. I was just wishing there was something I could do – anything that would stop her from crying like that. It makes me feel all wrong inside when grown-ups cry – as if the world has somehow turned upside down. And then suddenly I knew what to do and I wondered why I'd not thought of it before. Leaving them all fussing round little Michael, I ran across the court to old Mrs Legg's home, practically falling down the steps to her cellar in my eagerness to fetch her. She asked me a few questions about Michael's wound and I felt so stupid because I couldn't answer them properly. I'd not been able to bring myself to look closely at it.

When I ran back to the Brighams' Mrs Elias was standing at their open door, her long nose poking through. Wherever there is trouble, Mrs Elias is to be found. But I pushed past her and told Mrs Brigham what I'd done. Mother, of course, didn't want anything to do with it. "You're not going to let that old witch meddle with your son's arm!" she cried, aghast. But Mrs Brigham put a hand gently on Mother's arm to quieten her and nodded to me to fetch Mrs Legg.

Tuesday 10 May

Called round to see Michael this evening. Already the angry redness in his arm has subsided a little and there's no fever. Such relief! I knew I'd never be able to forgive myself if anything had happened to him. But I needn't have worried, for as soon as she saw me Mrs B gave me such a warm hug and thanked me over and over again and I knew then that Michael was all right.

Jack and Mr B came in just as I was leaving. Jack came straight up to me and told me that he was sorry for what he'd said to me before. "I'll never forget what you did for Michael," he said. Then he smiled shyly at me. "I couldn't bear to have lost my brother," he said suddenly in a low voice. He wasn't looking at me but I felt sure he was thinking of William and the terrible day he'd collapsed at the mill. We sat on the step together and I listened while he told me quietly how much he missed William. How important their friendship had been. Though we've known the Brighams a long time, I've always thought of Jack as William's friend. But as we talked, I forgot to feel shy. It was so good to talk to someone who really misses him like me. Went to bed happy, remembering William, thinking of Jack.

Wednesday 11 May

Went down to Mr Owen's this evening. Bought tea and sugar for Mother and bread and candles for the Brighams. Little Michael was restless last night and Mrs Brigham doesn't like to leave his side. On the way home I ran into Mrs Elias, out with her two children. She put her hand on my arm, thrust her face up close and told me how sorry she was to hear that we'd had to leave school. Then she said that the pawnbroker would have the shirt off her back before she'd let *her* children miss their schooling. Her words upset me so much that I backed away as fast as I could, and it was that, I think, which made me take a wrong turning. Next thing I knew I was outside Mr Brown's bookshop. I quickened my step as I neared it – I don't like Mr Brown or his shop. It's so dirty that you can scarcely see the books for all that grime and mould growing in the windows. But Mr Brown must have heard me for he scuttled to the door and had it open quick as a flash. He beckoned to me with a grubby finger. Slowly, I went up to him.

"Your father hasn't been in for his *Star* recently," he said, those little round glasses of his slipping down his long nose. I backed off a little, my skin shrinking. There's a funny sort of smell about Mr Brown, a damp, mouldy smell from living so near the canal.

"N-no," I stammered, no idea what he was on about.

"I can't keep ordering it for him, you know," he went on, edging his bony face up nearer mine. Long strands of hair swung like seaweed round his face.

"Tell him," he said, as I ran off. "You tell him."

I turned round and saw him dancing up and down, waving his fist after me and screeching like an old crow. I bunched up my skirts so that I could run faster, ignoring the shouts and whistles of the children playing amongst the ruined houses near the canal. As I ran, I wondered what the *Star* was.

At supper, I told Father what Mr Brown had said. But as soon as I mentioned the *Star* Mother exploded. "You're not still wasting our money on that Chartist rubbish," she cried, her cheeks reddening. "You know we've none to throw away." She was so angry that I think she forgot that Emmy, me and Grandfather were also at the table. "How many times have I told you that those Chartists will bring us nothing but trouble."

Father kept his head down, eating. Emmy looked

round the table smiling. I longed to wipe that smirk off her face. "Answer me now," said Mother imperiously.

I wished I'd never mentioned that wretched *Star* for at that Father pushed back his chair and got up from the table. "Don't you dare go out," cried Mother.

"I'm just going to see how little Michael does," he said quietly.

My cheeks felt red hot. I didn't touch a morsel, I felt that bad inside. Later I asked Father about the Chartists, but he told me that I wouldn't understand and that it was best to leave such matters alone. Felt so cross then. I hate it when Father treats me like a child. And just how does he think I can forget something that upsets our family so much?

Thursday 12 May

Bert Elias strolled back into the court today as cool as you please. No one's seen him for days – not even Mrs Elias, I think. It was Emmy saw him first. She called to me and together we stared through the window and watched him disappear into the little house at the end of our court. Suddenly there was a great squawk and Emmy and I jumped and stuffed our aprons in our mouths, it sounded so funny. Then we heard shouts and cries and it stopped being funny. I looked round and saw doors open, windows pull up. Mother saw what we were about then and pulled us back from the window with one arm and slammed it down with the other. She gave us a right telling off for being so nosy, but I saw her face crease up with worry.

"That Bert," she said, shaking her head as she went round the house, flicking a cloth here, picking things up and putting them down again. I asked her what she meant and she just said shortly that Mrs Elias had a *lot* to put up with.

Jack didn't think it was funny either when I told him about it later. "He's a bad one, that Bert," he said. "Straight from the mill to the beerhouse most days." Then he blushed and looked embarrassed, as though he'd said too much. I couldn't get a word out of him after that. How does *Jack* know about the beerhouse?

It was very late before Mrs Elias's door opened again. I saw her hurry out through the court, a child grasped tightly in each hand. Right embarrassed she looked when she caught my eye. But I don't think it was just Bert on her mind. From the way she looked I feel sure her children'll have to leave school too.

Sunday 15 May

Father up and out again early this morning. We're becoming so used to his odd appearances and disappearances that we scarcely notice them any more. Usually I miss his quiet presence in the house but today I was relieved to see him go. Mother's still angry with him and when they're like this there's just not room in our little house for both of them. Saw poor Molly Armthwaite come out of her door and hurry past, a bundle in her arms. I get a sinking feeling every time I see the Armthwaites now – I keep thinking it could be us. That sounds selfish I know, but I can't help it. Whose turn's it next to be spat out by the mill when it's done with them?

Whit Monday 16 May

Early this morning Mother took Emmy and me to see the Sunday-school children weave their way through the streets to church. They do this every Whitsuntide. They take it in turns. Mondays it's the Anglicans, then other faiths on other days. They were all dressed in spotless white, and some carried garlands of spring flowers. They looked so beautiful! Mother was almost in tears as we watched; I could tell how much she had hoped that we could join them. Her grandfather had been a churchwarden and she's so proud of him. It's because of Father we don't go to church. His family were all staunch chapel-goers, Mother says – not that I've seen either him or Grandfather inside a chapel for a fair while now.

Mindful of what we are missing, Mother sent me and Emmy down to Mr Owen's for buns and gingerbread. Then she sent me next door to ask the Brighams to join us. But Mrs Brigham wouldn't leave little Michael's side, so I took round buns and gingerbread and had my tea with them.

Tuesday 17 May

Mother lost patience with me again this morning. She held up the shirt I was patching and we both looked at the puckered stitching. I tried to concentrate while she showed me how to do it, but my thoughts kept drifting away. I could hear the shouts of children playing in our court and on the streets beyond. The schools are shut for the Whitsuntide holiday. It was not just the children distracting me, mind. I'm just not interested! And, oh, how I miss school. There's so much more I want to learn – not just sewing and cleaning and keeping house. I told Grandfather how I felt and he thought for a minute. "School isn't the only place you can learn," he said at last. "Knowledge is to be found in many places – even in stones, and in the trees and flowers of the field." I love Grandfather dearly, but sometimes he says the most peculiar things!

Wednesday 18 May

This afternoon Grandfather asked Mother if he could borrow my arm for a while. Mother nodded, biting the end off a bit of thread. I don't think she even heard him. He winked at me and put his finger to his lips and I felt all excited then as though we were going on a secret expedition together. I was so pleased when I saw that he was taking me to Mrs Legg's. I love visiting her home – it's a real treasure trove. Full of the oddest things – little pots of ointments and poultices all lined up on her mantelpiece, and the boxes that she uses for table and chairs. Bundles of flowers and herbs hanging off nails in the ceiling and walls to dry. Often there's a pot of them bubbling on her fire. Today there was such a sweet smell coming from them. But I couldn't see Mrs Legg – that little room is so dark. Just one tiny window, and that so high up in the wall that only a little light ever manages to straggle through. But as my eyes got used to it I could see what looked like a bundle of rags huddled on a box next to the fireplace. Then the bundle stirred and I realized that it was Mrs Legg. She got up and hobbled towards us and I was amazed how fast she could move her bent and bony body. Grandfather smiled at her and handed her a package and I watched as she unwrapped it, tearing off the paper in her eagerness to open it. Inside was a thick piece of bacon. Mrs Legg squealed and gave Grandfather a big hug. The sheet of newspaper still lay crumpled on the floor where it had fallen and as I bent down to pick it up, I saw the words on it. *The Northern Star* – written at the top in big black letters.

The Northern Star! It was that Chartist paper of Father's. I looked at it eagerly, but before I could read any more, a hand reached down quickly and scooped the paper up. "Your fire has nearly gone out," said Grandfather. "Let's see if this will help get it going again." There was nothing I could do but sit and stare as the paper curled into the flames.

We sat close together and I pretended to listen as they talked. But my mind was on that newspaper. Where had it come from? Had Grandfather taken it to stop Mother finding it in the house? After we left I asked Grandfather to tell me what he knew about the Chartists but he just said he'd learned that it was best to leave politics to politicians. And when I asked him to explain he said that I was asking too many questions and that I'd do better to listen to Mrs Legg. Sometimes I feel as though something is afoot in our town and the Chartists are behind it. Else what is the reason for all this mystery? One thing's for sure – I'll burst and soon if I don't find out about them somehow.

Friday 20 May

Feeling a bit bothered today. I think that something's being kept from me. Not about the Chartists this time – something else. Sometimes when Father gets home I catch him giving Mother these funny looks and then I see them both glance at me but as soon as they see I've seen they smile and pretend that everything's fine. But it's not, I know it's not.

Saturday 21 May

Something terrible has happened. I can scarcely bring myself to write the words. I AM TO START AT THE MILL ON MONDAY. I can't believe it, I just can't. "You said never," I cried to Mother, flinging back the words she'd said when little Michael was injured.

Her face was white. "Oh, Eliza," she said. "I'm so sorry. So very sorry. If there was anything I could have done... I've tried and tried to find work for myself but..." I saw her spread out her hands in a helpless sort of way.

"Where am I to work?" I demanded. The room was so quiet that I could hear myself breathe. I was terrified as I waited for Father to answer. What if I was to become a piecer. Like Jack. Like William. How would I ever manage to piece together the broken threads on a mule like Father's. I'm all fingers and thumbs! Or operate the weaving loom as Mother used to do. Four of them I think she had to look after.

"In the carding room," Father said at last. "Sickness. They need more hands."

"Cheap hands more like," said Mother, bitterly.

I stood there, watching them as they argued. Father stubborn, telling Mother how much we needed the money; Mother saying that he'd failed us, let the family down. I hardly heard them, I felt so far away. I felt as though it wasn't really me they were talking about. As if I wasn't Eliza any more, just a pair of hands. Factory hands.

Sunday 22 May

We went to Green Heys Fields this afternoon. "A breath of country air will do us all good," Mother said. I hardly cared. Ever since they told me I'd be going to the mill I've felt numb inside.

We all went – even Father found time to join us. I lay in the sweet-smelling grass and looked up at the sky but all I could see and smell was the smoke and steam belching out of the mill chimney. In my ears the caw of the rooks sounded like the clatter of the machines. I felt as though great walls were closing in on me. Dear Grandfather tried to rouse me by asking me to pick comfrey and sweet woodruff to take home to Mrs Legg. I got up then and helped him, stinging my hands on nettles as I reached in for the flowers. Tomorrow I will walk through the big gate to the mill. How will I bear it?

Monday 23 May

Am so tired, I can scarcely bear to write at all, and my legs and arms ache so much. Mother took one look at me when I came though the door this evening and told me to go upstairs to rest. But I wouldn't, not until I'd cleaned away the dirt – the fluff that still clung to me, the oil staining my hands and feet. Afterwards, I must have fallen asleep because I woke to find someone shaking my shoulder and I was terrified it was morning again. But it was only Mother, waking me for supper. I followed her downstairs, but I could hardly get anything down. Those big machines still haunt me. I had to stand behind them and watch the slivers of cotton unreel into the large cans. They're four feet tall – nearly as big as me. My hands were shaking so much at first that I thought I'd drop them. And the endless sweeping and cleaning. And all the time, longing to sit down – even for a minute. And that smell of oil and sweat, and the fluff that gets into the water and even on to your food. But worst is knowing that tomorrow I'll have to go there again.

Tuesday 24 May

Just as tired today. But I'm determined to write down all I can about my first day at the mill. I *need* to tell someone, and who else can I truly confide in?

I got woken early – five o'clock, Father said when I asked him. Mother was already up by the time I was dressed, and when I went down she grabbed my arm and rubbed a wet cloth across my face and hands. "That will do for now," she said, "but mind, you must wash properly on Thursday and next Monday." Then I had some tea that Mother had warmed up for us and there were oatcakes with a dab of butter on the table. But I hardly had time to get a mouthful down. Already I could hear the sound of doors opening and closing and the clapping of clogs across the court. It felt so strange to think I'd be joining them. I stood there in a daze while Mother gave me a quick hug and pressed a hunk of bread and fat bacon into Father's and my hands before pushing us towards the door.

The cold air made me gasp and now I felt fully awake. My stomach churning, as we joined the other hands clattering into the yard. Father took me straight to the carding room and handed my certificate to Mr Davis, the overlooker. It's to show my age. By law he can't work me more than twelve hours in any day. Mr Davis is in charge of the carding room, but oh, how I wish he wasn't. He's *always* shouting. I've already noticed he's got it in for one little girl. Mary Whittle's her name. She looks even more scared than me.

I was put to work with a carder called Annie. It's her job to feed the carding machine with the cleaned cotton. I think she must be quite old, for there's white in her hair and it's not from the fluff that gets on our hair and clothes. She didn't say much, but quickly she showed me what to do and told me that I must put up my hair and roll up my sleeves in case they get caught in the machines. I'd already noticed that everyone had kicked off their clogs when they came in for the floor is slippy with oil. We took off our shawls too before we started work, and some of the women tied their jackets round their throats. It gets quite warm in that room though it is not nearly as bad as the spinning room.

Was so tired by dinnertime. If Annie hadn't shared her pie with me I'd have gone hungry for I had no money to buy my own. Felt so ashamed when I told her, and so weary that only pride held back my tears. I said that Mother had expected me to go home for my dinner, but that I had not enough time now. Twelve hours I'm supposed to work. Twelve hours! I didn't get the full breaks, and even after the bell had gone I was still stuck in that carding room. But Mr Davis doesn't seem to care – certificate or no certificate. And there's *nothing* I can do about it. I can't imagine I'll ever get used to this, whatever hours I do, and I think my poor legs and arms ache even worse than they did yesterday.

Wednesday 25 May

Mother gave me a penny to buy my dinner today. It was as well that she did, for again I didn't have a full hour's break and there's no time to return home for my meal. Mother's so angry that Mr Davis keeps me back to clean, but there's little she can do. If she complains I may be dismissed, and we need my wages so much.

And then there are the fines – one for each rule in the list pinned up on the wall. Twopence, just for leaving waste unswept. The same for being five minutes late back to work. There are even rules about how often we wash. At least twice a week we must do this – Monday and Thursday mornings, as Mother said. That means I'll have to wake even earlier on those days for you're fined three whole pence if you don't wash properly. But Annie says that so long as I arrive on time, keep my eyes on the machine and my nose clean I'll do all right.

Annie is kind. I think I'm lucky to work alongside her. Some of the carders treat their assistants ever so badly – like that Matilda. She's a big woman with a rough tongue and a hand to go with it, and often I see her little assistant in tears. A half-timer poor Sam is. Nine hours in the mill and then two at the mill school. Annie says that the teacher can barely write his name and that poor Sam may as well spend those hours asleep for all the learning he'll get there. But Annie's different. When we broke for dinner today, she went to fetch me a cup of water to ease the tickle in my throat. I've been coughing and spluttering a lot today. The water she brought me though – it hadn't been changed for a while, and it was full of fluff and I had to pick it out before I could drink it. There's a wheel at one end of the room that's supposed to make a draught and free the air of dust, but it's broken and the air is full of the flyings as Annie calls it. The floor's covered with the stuff too.

Every bit of the waste cotton is swept up and gets used and often the big machines are still moving as we clean. This afternoon I was in such a hurry I nearly slipped on the sticky floor and into the massive machine, and this seemed to cause the other girls much amusement. They think I'm stuck-up and I feel sure they're dying to get me into trouble with Mr Davis. It's hard to do what Annie says and ignore them. And whenever I look up I see Mr Davis watching me, and my hands feel even bigger and clumsier than usual. I'm sure that one day I'll fall over with one of the large cans in my arms, the slivers will unwind all over the oily floor and I'll be dismissed.

Thursday 26 May

Father gets woken by the knocker-up rattling his long pole against the windows, but I never hear a sound until suddenly there is Father's voice buzzing in my ear, his hand shaking my shoulder. He says that one day soon I'll learn to wake at the right hour for work. I can't imagine that time will ever come. I hate to see the fear in his eyes when I'm slow to wake, how nervous and jumpy he is, how fearful of being late. Father's one of the best spinners at the mill – his fingers are deft, and the cotton he spins as fine as silk. He'd be such a loss to the mill. I just hope they realize it.

Today I noticed how drawn and tired Annie is looking. Like many of the carding-room hands she's much troubled by a nagging cough. She's thin too, and bloodless-looking like many of those here. She is bent and tallowy yellow, not pink like me – as though she's worked here for a long time. I'd thought she was quite old, but today she told me she's just 30.

Saturday 28 May

Today we worked only nine hours instead of twelve, and afterwards I hurried to join the other hands in the line for my first week's wages. When at last I came out into the yard, I saw Father standing near the gate. I watched him search for my face among all the other stragglers – the rovers, the slubbers, scavengers and piecers. Many of them are not much older than Emmy, with deep smudges of tiredness under their eyes. His face lit up when he saw me, and that big knot of anger I'd still been feeling melted a little. I even let him hug me and it was good to feel the warmth of his arms. He put up his hand to brush something off my hair and as the strands of white stuff floated to the ground, I fancied he was brushing the mill off me.

Mother welcomed us home and thanked me when I handed over my meagre wages. Three shillings and four pence! That was all I had to give them. But they took it with a flourish and put it in the pot as though I'd given them a handful of gold sovereigns. They told me that I should feel proud I'm able to help the family in hard times.

Sunday 29 May

Got up late and then helped Mother prepare a meal. Father said that it was the finest he'd ever tasted, and I saw him smile at me as he said it. As if my pitiful wages had produced a feast! Buttered potatoes with some slivers of bacon and tea to follow. After I'd helped Mother clear the dishes away, Emmy pulled at my apron and asked me to play with her, but I sent her away telling her to amuse herself with the other children. I felt sorry for what I'd said when I saw her hurt face, but I have not enough energy even for play. When I get more used to the long hours, maybe I'll be able to study again – but I can't really imagine it.

Monday 30 May

The rest yesterday did me good and I'd even woken before Father came up this morning. But how the day dragged! This afternoon I found myself dreaming about the day I'd return to school. Not as a pupil now, mind – but as a teacher. A sharp slap awoke me from my daydream. One of the cans was full and the thick slivers overflowing. I rushed to fetch an empty one, feeling the sharp sting still on my cheek. I dare not daydream. Every few minutes I have to replace the full cans with empty ones. Those machines don't all stop until the bell rings for dinner. Often they're still clattering away when we grab a few minutes' break for breakfast.

This evening Father told us that Lever's mill is to stop working. Now even the young Armthwaites will be without work. Mother says that Bill Armthwaite has no choice but to go to the Board to ask for help. It's that or the workhouse for them, she says – "if they can fit them in," she added darkly. But Father told us they'll send Bill to work in the stone yard. He's a strong man, he says. I don't know that Bill Armthwaite's that strong – bow-legged and hollow-chested he looks to me – just like most spinners get after a time. But strong enough to spoil his hands for a few shillings a week. I can remember bad times before, but none as bad as these. Much as I hate it, I pray that our mill does not close. I don't know what we'd do if it did.

Wednesday 1 June

Emmy's got into the habit of following me around when I get home nowadays, and I have trouble finding a peaceful moment to write. She comes upstairs after me and I see her eyes dart suspiciously around our room. It's as if she's guessed I'm keeping something from her. I know she wonders what I do up here all the time on my own. Sometimes she comes in when I'm writing and then I don't even have time to put the diary back in the hiding place I've found for it under one of the loose floorboards, and I stuff it under the blanket till she's gone. This diary is *my* secret and I've not told a soul about it – not even Jack. And when I'm up in that little room, often I don't feel as if I'm on my own at all. That sounds so odd, I know, but it's the strangest thing – more and more I've been feeling as if William is back. Especially when I write my diary. Perhaps because sometimes I feel as if I'm talking to *him* when I write. Often he seems so real. As if he's sitting beside me again. I hold my breath and I almost think I hear him next to me. And then I realize I'm being silly and the feeling goes, and I feel so alone and miserable again.

Sunday 5 June

The Armthwaites left this morning. They've gone to stay with their cousins who live a little way north of Ancoats. They're going to stay there until Bill finds work. I've seen their cousins when they've come to visit – another large family. How they'll all fit into the one small house I can't imagine. I watched through the bedroom window as the handcart was loaded up with their few possessions. It made my chest contract to see it. The noise had woken Mother too. I saw her hurry out of the house just as Bill Armthwaite was picking up the shafts. It was very early and there was no one else up to see them leave – not even that nosy Mrs Elias. Mother hurried round to the back of the cart where Molly Armthwaite stood, one hand on the cart, the other in a young boy's.

With a jolt, Bill pulled the cart forward and the children swayed and clung on tightly to the sides. I saw them giggle and bounce about in their seats as it jolted over the potholes. They looked all excited, just as if they were going on a big adventure. Mother kept her arm round Molly Armthwaite as the cart slowly bumped out of the narrow entrance of the court. All the way out of the court Molly had her head down.

It was only as we sat to our breakfast that I realized Father was out again. I don't think Mother even noticed. We were in such a daze all day long – our thoughts full of the Armthwaites.

Tuesday 7 June

My worst day at the mill *ever*. Even worse than my first day, and when I got home I was still trembling with the horror of it. I went upstairs at once, praying that Emmy wouldn't follow me, but she did, and I didn't want to talk to her. I didn't want to talk to anyone – not even Grandfather and least of all Emmy. I snapped at her to leave and she burst out howling and ran down the stairs and I could hear her wail to Mother. Then Mother shouted up the stairs at me but her voice sounded so far away. Much clearer in my head was Mary's scream, as clear as if I was still in the carding room and even when I shut my eyes now I can see the look in Sam's eyes when Matilda went for him.

It was late this afternoon it happened, after Mother had been and left my tea. I'd seen Sam's head nod on his chest and then he jerked it up. Then it began to nod again and slowly he toppled forwards. No one else seemed to have noticed and I found I couldn't speak, the words just wouldn't come. I couldn't leave the machines but I only had one eye on them, mind, the other was fixed on Sam as he toppled towards the wire teeth of that great carding machine. Then I heard a shout and Matilda's hand reached down and grabbed Sam back. You might have thought Mr Davis would be worried but he wasn't, he was angry. He yelled at Matilda and at Sam, and later I saw Matilda cuff poor Sam round the ears while he cowered near the machine, his arms wrapped round his head. Matilda's face had gone all red and angry. I can't truly believe Sam's as much as nine, his legs are so spindly, they look as though they'll snap.

After that, it was little Mary Whittle's turn. We all know that Mr Davis has got it in for her and I feel certain she can't be nine either. Mary helps with the cleaning and bringing the cleaned cotton to the carding machines – odd jobs like that. She always looks so tired as she wobbles up to the machines, back bent under the loads of cotton.

Anyway, today she slipped, the cotton fell on to the floor with a thump and Mr Davis was across the floor in a bound and had her by the hair. He yanked her up and I heard her scream as he dragged her across the room. One of the other children who'd come in with Mary scuttled round the floor trying to sort out the mess. If I could, I'd have shut my eyes so tight I wouldn't have had to see poor Mary's face, but I know I'd never have been able to shut out the sound of her cries.

Friday 10 June

Tomorrow I finish my third week at the mill. Annie told me she was pleased with me. Said I'm quick and hard working. I told her I've noticed Mr Davis no longer watches me so closely. But her words give me no comfort. I want my old life back!

Saturday 11 June

Emmy upset today. Mother had found a bit of meat for our tea, but when Emmy saw it she burst out howling, pushed her plate away across the table, and said she wouldn't touch it. As soon as her crying had reached the hiccuping stage we managed to get out of her what was wrong. It seems she's heard that there are people who've been forced to eat dead dogs. There's nothing else for them to eat, she cried. It's that or starve. I thought I'd choke, it was so funny. Emmy *really* thought that Mother had given us dog to eat! I told her not to be so silly, but Mother shot me a furious look. I stuffed my apron into my mouth and tried to be quiet. But even Father's lips were twitching I could see. It turns out that there are these posters all round the town talking about this family who've had the choice between eating dog or going without. Father says the posters are the work of the Anti Corn Law League. I looked puzzled and asked him what that was. He thought for a minute and then said: "The Anti Corn Law League think that if they swapped the dog for a loaf of bread everything would be all right." I thought he must be joking! There was a rare twinkle in his eyes as he spoke, so I think he was just trying to cheer us up. But *I'd* gone off my food now too, and I heard Mother exclaim as I pushed my plate away from me. But it wasn't just the thought of food that made my stomach churn. I was thinking about that family on the posters. Was it true what it said? Did that poor family really have to eat dog?

Father didn't say, but the way things are in this town, I wouldn't be surprised.

Sunday 12 June

I've found out at last about the Chartists and I could burst with wanting to talk to someone about them. It was this afternoon. I'd gone out on an errand for Mother – she'd asked me to take a package to Mrs Barlow, an old neighbour who used to live in our court. As I left she'd told me to hurry for the streets were no place for a girl to dawdle in. "I'd take it myself but my hands are full with Emmy," she said worriedly. "And I can't ask your grandfather to walk so far. But I know I can trust my big girl," and with that she gave me a quick peck on the cheek. I think that was to make me feel better, but if I hadn't been so glad to get out of the house I'd have felt annoyed. Emmy had woken with a cold and aching head this morning, but from the fuss Mother was making you'd think she was in a consumption! Anyway, I made sure to heed her words and walked quickly at first, but it was a fine hot day, the streets were full of people and soon I found myself dawdling.

It was when I was about to turn off for Mrs Barlow's that I saw them. The banners! Streaming through the air and just about to disappear down the next street. "O'Connor – the Champion of the People" one said. Another had the words: "No Surrender". The third was borne so high I couldn't see what it said at first, but then the wind licked it back towards me and I saw the words clearly: "The Charter". Before I knew what I was doing my feet were following those banners. Street after street I turned down. Where I was or where I was going I scarcely knew – and then I found myself in a broad thoroughfare and at the back of an enormous crowd of people. Then suddenly the crowd parted and I felt myself pushed back – almost crushed so I could hardly breathe. Ahead of me I saw a group of men stride through the parting crowd. The man leading them was dressed just like Father in fustian jacket and trousers, but I felt sure he was no working man. There was such fire in his eyes and I felt a strange excitement rise inside me. I looked around. There were a lot of women in the crowd. Many of them were wearing green ribbons in their hair and I think some of them must have felt a bit like me. They were crying – but it wasn't because they were sad. I almost felt like crying too, though I hardly knew why. And then I felt a hand grip my arm and pull me backwards out of the crowd. I tried to shake it off. "Eliza, what are you doing here?" a voice hissed. It was Jack!

I wanted to ask *him* the same question! Jack said that it was not safe for me to be there – that he'd take me home. I told him he would have to drag me there first. That I knew well these people were Chartists and I'd not leave until he told me *everything*. And that I wanted to know who that man in the fustian jacket was, and why all those women were wearing green ribbons. "First, you must promise me you will not say a word of what I tell you," he said. "Not to anyone." He looked so solemn that I was hard put not to laugh, but I gave him my word. I was right, they were Chartists and green was a Chartist colour. They had come to hear Fergus O'Connor speak.

I remembered the words I'd seen on the banner: O'Connor – the Champion of the People. That was the man in the fustian jacket. "He is not like other gentlemen," said Jack. "Not like the masters. He truly believes in the rights of working men and cares more for that than anything else." I looked at Jack astonished. He'd spoken so fiercely. "Why were you so afraid to tell me this?" I asked him.

"Because many of the masters dismiss anyone they suspect of being a Chartist," Jack said. He told me that the Chartists are fighting for the People's Charter to become the law of the land. "The Charter demands that every working man be given the right to vote, Eliza. Then we'll be able to elect a government who'll listen to us. They'll learn what our lives are really like. When that happens, the masters will lose their power to control our lives. They'll not give up that power easily."

He didn't mention working women I noticed. Were they not to get the vote too? "One day," Jack said when I asked him, "but we must go step by step." Some Chartists were all for women's rights, but most still felt it was enough for men to have the vote. He told me then that a great petition had been signed by the Chartists and taken to Parliament in May. "It needed sixteen strong men to carry it, Eliza. It was so big they couldn't get it through the door and it had to be broken up to be got into the building. Over three million ordinary people signed that petition," he said. "Think on that."

From the way he was looking at me I knew, as clearly as if he'd said the words, that my father's name was amongst them. I didn't know what I felt then. Excited I think, but frightened too. "Last month Parliament turned our petition down," he said. "They are frightened too – frightened of the Charter. But one day Parliament will listen to us. They'll have to," he added fiercely.

If over three million could not make them change their mind what would? "Chained to the machine we are and always will be," I said. "We'll *never* escape them."

"It is not the machines but the work," said Jack. "The bad wages we get for it. That's what we *must* change."

But how? I thought again. The Charter sounded a glorious thing, but as I looked at the great heaving mass of people around me I felt scared too. I tried to imagine what would happen if all these people decided they'd had enough. Enough of poor pay, of seeing their children go hungry. And then I remembered Father's words about the Anti Corn Law League. So much is going on in this town – so much bubbling away below the surface. Like a great cauldron coming fast to the boil.

As we walked home Jack said again that I must tell no one what I'd learned today. Not even my family. That it is hard to know who to trust. His words bother me greatly.

Mother was furious when I got back. I'd quite forgotten my errand and she asked me where I thought I'd been all this time. She gave Jack a pretty odd look too, though she thanked him for bringing me home. She had been out of her mind with worry she told me. "The streets are no place for a girl to dawdle these days," she said. "Have you no sense?" I think I'll be upstairs for a very long time, for nothing will drag the truth out of me.

I can scarcely see to write but I'll try. I'm hoping that if I write my fears down perhaps I'll be able to make sense of them. Perhaps they'll even go away. It's Father. It was late when he came in and as soon as he did Mother started. Emmy and I clearly heard her shout that she knew full well where he'd been, and that she was sick of the Chartists and that he'd lose his job if he didn't show more sense. "That piecer of yours will get your job," she cried, "and we will all be turned out on to the streets." Emmy was in tears and I told her that there was nothing to worry about, but I didn't really believe it. Deep down I feel sure Father would never do anything to risk his job, but why else would Mother shout at him like that? And then I thought about what Jack told me this afternoon – about the

Charter and that petition and what might happen if the master found out Father had signed it...

Saturday 18 June

After I'd got back from work today Mother took Emmy and me down to the market. Usually I love to loiter at the little stalls, but today my eyes were caught by the posters that were plastered everywhere. Not just talking about families feeding off dogs, but something else just as bad. "Public Peace in Danger from Starvation in Manchester," they said in bold black letters. I wanted to stop and read them, for I felt sure that these were Chartist posters, but when Mother saw what I was doing she seized my arm and pulled me away. She's still cross with me. I'm surprised she's thawed enough to let me out of doors!

After that she kept my arm in such a firm grip and walked so fast that my aching legs could scarcely keep up with her. And then I saw Mrs Legg. Her head was bent so low it nearly brushed the ground. In one hand she held a sack and the fingers of the other searched for scraps dropped near the stalls. I heard a soft thump near me. A stallholder had dropped something on the ground. Mrs Legg gave a cry of triumph. There, by her feet, lay a beautiful fresh cabbage. I watched as she leaned forward to scoop it up into her sack. But just as the wrinkled fingers were about to pick it up, a grubby hand shot out from under the stall and seized it from her. I was so angry that anyone could do such a thing to poor old Mrs Legg that I reached down to grab it back.

I found myself staring into the eyes of one of the Armthwaite children. She looked back at me for a minute – right defiant that look of hers was – and then scuttled away under the stalls, the cabbage held tightly in her dirty apron. I thought of the words on the poster and I felt as if a big hand was squeezing my stomach. I pulled at Mother's arm urgently. "What is it now, Eliza?" she snapped. I told her who I'd seen, and Mother looked at me closely. "Are you sure?" she said. She sounded doubtful and for a moment I almost doubted myself – there are so many hungry children on the streets. But I was certain. "Where is she now?" Mother questioned. I said I did not know, but that she'd looked so dirty and hungry. I could hear my voice wobble – I felt close to tears.

Sunday 19 June

Mother went to see the Armthwaites today. Very grim she looked when she got back. But she wouldn't talk about her visit. I think of Jack's fierce words about the Chartists, but what can *they* do, what can anyone do to help people like Mrs Legg and the Armthwaites? It will take more than fine words, I think, to fill *their* bellies.

Wednesday 22 June

Saw Jack in the mill yard after work and ran up to him. He smiled and asked how I was. "Ooh look," I heard a voice behind me say. "Our Eliza has got a sweetheart. What will owd Annie have to say." Much to my annoyance, I found myself blushing, and when I looked round at Jack I saw that his ears were pink –

and next minute he'd gone. It's our old bond to William that has drawn Jack and me closer together – that's all. When I got home I told Mother what had happened. "Jack's a steady lad," she said carefully. "But not everyone knows he's an old friend. Folk might talk if they see you about together."

Thursday 23 June

One of the girls in the carding room was fined today. She burst into tears when Mr Davis tapped his cane at the list of rules, and whispered that she could not read. Not that Mr Davis cared! I felt so sorry for her, but shocked too that a girl of fifteen or sixteen can't read. I told Annie that I would be ashamed to be so ignorant, but Annie told me not to be so critical. Many of the girls here began work when they were very young – they'd no chance to learn. She gave a strange sort of smile when she said that, and I asked her how she'd come to start work. She said she'd begun when she was very little. Her parents had not wanted to send her to the mill, but times were hard and they'd no choice. When *she* was young, mills employed children even younger than my little sister.

I was so surprised, for Annie is not like the other women who work here. It's hard to believe she's had so little schooling. I asked her if she minded. She shrugged and said that she'd had no choice. As I sit here, my aching legs propped up on the dresser drawer to rest, I find that I can't put Annie's words out of my head. They make me feel so frightened. When I look at Annie I see a woman worn out, broken down by the machine, then suddenly, it's not Annie I see but myself – in fifteen years' time.

Monday 27 June

Felt so sick when I woke this morning. I've been feeling sick quite a bit on and off these past days. It's like something's twisting inside my stomach and it's not just nerves – I know that. Father had a rare struggle to get me up, and then I retched up some of the fluff from the carding. We walked slowly to the mill, and at the gate Father got me some hot tea and made me drink it before we went in. I could tell that he was trying not to show his worry, mind – hopping from foot to foot he was, as the hands pushed past us into the mill. So I drank it fast as I could, feeling it scald my insides all the way down to my poor stomach, which felt as though it'd been kicked.

Just got into the carding room in time! Mr Davis gave me his usual welcoming scowl and Annie a worried look, but when she later went to get me some water I pulled a face and pushed it away. I felt I'd sooner suffer a parched throat than drink that muck.

I told Annie that I'd been sick and how odd my stomach felt. "That'll be the fluff," she said. "Some folk don't mind swallowing it – makes them feel full when they've a bit of a hunger coming on." Her words made me feel bad all over again. I hate the water here. But by the middle of this afternoon, thirst won over and anyway there's so much of the stuff in the air, it makes little odds.

Wednesday 29 June

Annie's been coughing badly this week but today she was much worse. She had a bottle of physic in her pocket and when she could she took it out and had a sip. She says that it eases her throat, but soon I heard her coughing again, clinging to the sides of the machine for support. Poor Annie. It's hard for her to mind the machines when she has to stop and cough so often. Mr Davis's eye was on her more and more frequently too. I'm so afraid she'll be dismissed. Country air – that's what Annie needs. I will ask Mrs Legg if she'll make me a poultice for Annie's chest.

Thursday 30 June

Annie didn't come to work. Mr Davis has ordered one of the assistants to take her place. Sarah, her name is. She's a solidly built girl with blank eyes who goes about her work with a bored look, and as soon as the bell goes, sits down with a novelette. I watched her finger follow the words slowly across the page. She scarcely said a word to me. As the day drew on I felt more and more frantic. Would Annie be fined heavily for her absence, or even dismissed? I feared that she was ill and had been unable to send word to Mr Davis.

When the bell rang this evening Mr Davis was called out of the room. When he got back he beckoned to Sarah. Before I left I asked her what he'd said. "Owd Annie's been taken to the Royal Infirmary," she said. "Her sister came for an infirmary order."

That's where they took William when he fell ill. I feel a sort of shrinking inside me when I think of going back to that terrible place. But I must – for Annie's sake.

Saturday 2 July

Went to see Annie at the hospital. It's a fair way from Ancoats, but it didn't seem long before I was walking up the wide entrance steps, great columns each side, all the time longing to turn and run. There was a gaggle of nurses inside and as I walked up to them one of them heard me and turned round. "What do you want?" she snapped. I told her why I was there and she took me over to the surgeon in charge of Annie's ward. The surgeon was bending over a patient and when he straightened up and wiped his hands on his apron I could see that it was bloodstained. But his eyes were kind, and he came up to me straight away. He told me I couldn't see Annie for she was asleep and then he asked me who I was. I could see in his face that he'd already guessed I was a mill girl. He said bluntly that Annie must find other work to do for her lungs cannot cope with the atmosphere in the carding room.

"I know, mister," I said. "The fluff has wound round her lungs and poisoned them. She needs to get away from the town into the countryside. She needs rest and fresh air."

I couldn't bear to stay any longer in that place and hurried away, but as I walked out on to that broad street again, I gasped. The gaslights had been lit and I felt as if I'd stepped into another world. So many fine carriages were rolling down the street and stopping at that smart hotel opposite the infirmary. I couldn't stop staring at it – at all the rich folk being helped out of their carriages and walking up the carpeted steps into the brilliant light. You'd never have known from looking at them that there was any trouble in Manchester, and after what I'd just seen it sickened me. And then I caught sight of a girl in a polished glass window and I stopped to look more closely. She had lank brown hair straggling round her face, her dress was patched with pieces of cotton fluff clinging to her like down. I was shocked. And then I knew who it was and stepped back. It was *me*. And yet it wasn't. That dirty, dishevelled girl. It just *couldn't* be me.

A man came to the door of the shop. "Be off with you now," he said. "I don't want any vagrants here." At that I picked up my skirts and I ran. I didn't stop until I got home.

As soon as I was back, I ran down to the tap to fill the bucket with water and then I scrubbed and scrubbed. But however hard I washed I felt that I'd never get rid of that girl. At last Mother stopped me and asked me what I thought I was doing. I burst into tears then. It was as if I couldn't hold it in any longer – all I'd been feeling these last weeks, it just burst out of me, and I leaned against her and sobbed and sobbed. She just stood there stroking my hair and saying nothing. But I felt she understood.

Monday 4 July

It's so hot outside, and hotter still in the carding room, and as soon as the dinner bell goes we rush outside and sit in the yard. I feel so sorry for Father and the Brighams. The spinning room is far hotter than the carding room and as the spinners and piecers come out for dinner they loosen neckties and fan their red faces with their caps. Worst of all is the boiler room, where the steam engine is fed with coal. The boilerman is purple by the time he totters out for his dinner. That boiler is on even before we come in in the morning – it has to be so that he can get enough power up to drive the machines by the time the bell goes.

How I miss Annie. Sarah is nice enough but we've nothing to say to each other. At dinner today I saw her in the yard, her nose stuck in one of those novelettes of hers. That girl called Biddy joined her and I watched them laugh and talk away, their legs swinging, pointing and giggling as they stared at the lads coming out of the spinning room. As I watched them, eating my dinner on my own, I felt lonelier and more miserable than ever. I know I have my diary, but oh, I wish I had someone to talk to, not just a shadow of one – a real person, solid, flesh and blood.

Friday 8 July

When Sarah was out of the room today I saw her book lying on the floor. I picked it up and opened it – just couldn't stop myself. I've been longing to know what it's about. Next thing I knew I felt this hand on my shoulder. I jumped in terror, fearing it was Mr Davis but it was only Sarah. Felt really awkward and gave her the book straight back but she smiled at me – a proper smile, the first time I've seen her do that – and told me I could borrow it if I liked. At dinnertime I joined her in the yard and she told me that she's soft on one of the piecers who works in the spinning room. Her face was all red but she wouldn't say who it is.

Sunday 10 July

Got up late and then spent the rest of the day hunched up in the window. I could not put that book down and Mother had to call several times to rouse me for tea. But when she saw my nose in a book she looked so pleased. I didn't dare show her what it is, mind. When I'd finished it, I hid it in the secret place where I keep my diary.

Monday 11 July

Finished the novelette Sarah lent me. "How quickly you read," she said admiringly. She's told me she'll bring me another tomorrow. I'm pleased for now I think I've found a way to forget all my troubles. Is that so very wrong?

Walked home today with Father and the Brighams. I was so glad to see Jack. I've taken care to avoid him these past weeks because of Mother, but I've missed his company. It's been lonely with neither him nor Annie to talk to.

Just before we turned into our court, Jack pulled me aside and whispered urgently that he'd nearly finished his invention and would I like to see it. I was so pleased that he wanted to show me! I looked at Father to see if I might go and he smiled and told me to run along.

I felt a bit stupid as I watched Jack run round his precious invention, eagerly showing me how it will work. I still did not know what to make of it. The candle was sputtering so much, it was hard to see anything in that cellar clearly. He's so proud of it – I think he'd like to spend all day building and repairing machines, but he'd need to train as a millwright or engineer, and the Brighams can't afford to pay for an apprenticeship. He told me that when the machine's finished he wants to take out a patent and sell it to the master of a mill works. He thinks it could pay for his training or that the master might give him a job in his workshop. "What about your father?" I asked him. "Doesn't he hope you'll become a spinner? Doesn't he want you to take over his wheels?"

Jack sighed. "Yes," he said. "But maybe Michael will when he's older. Now that his arm is mending so well, we think he'll be able to return to the mill one day soon."

He asked how I was getting along with my studying. I must have looked puzzled, for he explained. "Your father says that your nose is never out of a book." I felt myself go red then. I knew full well what Jack would think of the books I was reading.

"Is it a secret?" he teased. "Your father says that you're interested in healing and plants. And I know you've always loved the country. I've heard you say often enough that you'd like to live there."

His words reopened the wound I've been nursing all these long weeks.

"Father knows nothing about it," I said bitterly. "I hardly ever see him. He's never home." I pulled one of Sarah's novelettes out of my pocket and handed it to him. "This is what I'm reading. It's all I'm fit for now that I'm a mill girl."

Jack turned the little book over in his hands. *Evelina's Dream* it was called. "That's not true, Eliza. You're worth much more than this. You know you are." He dropped the book to the floor.

I turned away from him so that he'd not hear my next words. But he heard. He heard.

"I hate the mill. I hate working there. I wish I'd not had to leave school." The words were out before I could stop myself.

Jack looked at me. "You're thirteen now, aren't you? 'Course you had to leave." He shrugged and turned away. "You always were a dreamer," he said at last. "Perhaps that's why you've not noticed what is happening around you. Can't you see that there are people not as fortunate as you? People who are starving. There are many who'd be grateful for even *half* of what you bring home."

I think he had a lot more to say, but I couldn't stand to hear it. I stood up and made my way out of the cellar. I was nearly in tears, but I would not let him see how much he'd hurt me.

Wednesday 13 July

Didn't get home until late this evening. Sarah asked me to join her, Biddy and Millie, and together we went out into the Ancoats streets. We linked arms and strode along, singing at the tops of our voices. I didn't care who saw me, I didn't care what people thought. Biddy said I must join them again. She said it's silly to always go straight home after work. I told her that I couldn't stay out, for I had no money of my own to spend. Biddy looked shocked. She's a tall girl, with bold blue eyes and a big laughing mouth. "Doesn't your family let you keep *any* money?" she asked. When I said no, she said she wouldn't put up with that. All those long hours, she said, and nothing to show for it. She wanted to lend me some but I refused.

Then she snatched some sweets off a street seller's tray and handed them round to us. I saw how casually she tossed the sweet seller a coin. I can't remember when I'd last tasted anything so good. I sucked it slowly, feeling the sweet fruitiness flood my mouth. Biddy laughed and gave me another.

Mother had words to say when I got home but I didn't let them trouble me. Why shouldn't I have some fun too? Why should my life be all work, work, work? Jack Brigham thinks I am a thoughtless child. Well, then, I'll behave like one!

Sunday 17 July

Slipped out as early as I could this morning. Sarah had told me yesterday that they were going to the Fields, and asked me to join them. Somehow I felt sure Mother wouldn't like me to go so I'd told her that I was going to see Annie. Felt so guilty when I saw the pleased look on Mother's face that I felt myself flush. I told myself I'd go to the hospital before I came home. But the rain came on when we were out and we spent the morning lounging round the town again. Millie and Biddy teased Sarah every time a young man walked past. "Is that him?" they said. "Is that your sweetheart?" Sarah was blushing.

"Where's that nice-looking sweetheart of yours,

Eliza?" Biddy said. I told them I didn't have one. "Yes you do, we've seen you with him." They laughed and told me that I was blushing. I felt secretly pleased that they thought I had a sweetheart, though their words upset me too. I do not want to think about Jack Brigham.

When we parted I put my hand into my apron pocket for the poultice and physic Mrs Legg had made for Annie. But they weren't there – I'd forgotten them. I shrugged my shoulders as Biddy would do and sauntered home. Told myself that I'd visit Annie another day.

Wednesday 20 July

The master brought a party of visitors to see the steam engine today. Mind, we're not allowed to see it – not *us*, not the hands. It was at dinner we saw them, the master bowing and scraping as he led them out of the yard, gold watch and chain bouncing up and down on his stomach. From the look of him, you'd never know that times are so hard he cannot afford to pay us full wages. We'd crowded to the window to take a look and I heard Biddy scoff quietly when she saw them. Millie hushed her nervously, glancing round at Mr Davis. Millie is a little mouse of a girl with a frightened face who tags along behind Biddy. When he saw us, Mr Davis ordered us back from the window, but Biddy tossed her head and muttered that she didn't see why our dinner hour should be shortened for a party of stuck-up folk prancing around in silks and velvets. We all looked at her admiringly. Biddy takes such risks! I'd never dare to be so bold. Have asked Sarah to bring me another of her storybooks. I can't get enough of them.

Thursday 21 July

Two boys were caught climbing up the wall to see the steam engine today! It must have been those visitors the master brought that made them want to try.

We all saw them when we went out into the yard for our dinner, high up on the wall and clinging on to the window-frame, feet scrabbling for a toehold on the brickwork. Then there was a big cry and the first boy fell through the window! We all screamed when we saw! They say he nearly toppled over the guard into the engine itself, but his friend somehow managed to pull him back. Not surprised they were dismissed.

Saturday 23 July

I am in such trouble! As I sit here writing I can hear still their voices talking downstairs. Wondering what to do with me I should think. Oh, if only Mother hadn't seen me out on Great Ancoats Street! Singing and shouting. Behaving like a hoyden, Mother said.

It was Emmy who saw me first. I couldn't believe it when I heard her voice behind me. "Look, Mother, it's our Eliza!" she'd cried, and I'd nearly jumped out of my skin.

"Don't be daft," I'd heard Mother's voice say then.

"It is, Mother, look!" squeaked Emmy's voice.

I carried on as though nothing was happening. Then

Mother's voice pulled me up. "Eliza!" she said, so loud we all stopped short where we were. My face felt so hot and my legs shook so I could scarcely stand up. And then I felt this hand shoot out and seize mine. I felt so small and so ashamed that Biddy and Sarah had seen. I do not know how I'll ever be able to face them again. But I'm angry too – what do Mother and Father expect. I am just a mill girl after all!

Back at home I saw Mother and Father look at each other. Father's knuckles showed white where he gripped his chair. Emmy sat there throughout it all, lapping up my discomfort, until Mother sent her round to the Brighams. I have no doubt she'll tell them all what a bad girl I am. Even Jack will know about it soon enough.

Tell myself I don't care, but I do, I feel so alone. Even William seems far away from me now. William – whose presence was such a comfort to me as I wrote my diary. Now it's as if *he's* turned against me too.

Sunday 24 July

I am still in disgrace and spent the day in my room. Grandfather brought me my meals. He looks sad but he says nothing.

Monday 25 July

Needn't have worried what the girls at work thought about what happened. As we left this evening Biddy and Sarah asked me to go out with them again. "Tell your mother we'll be good," Biddy laughed. I shook my head and said that I was needed at home. But I could feel myself blush as I said it. I couldn't tell them the truth – that Mother has forbidden me to go out with them again. She says she'll give me such a walloping if she catches me out with those bad girls. I think they felt sorry for me and Biddy said that they were still my friends and squeezed my hand. Whatever Mother says, I know that they're not bad, not really. Now all I have is my diary.

Sunday 31 July

We had tea with the Brighams this afternoon. I didn't want to go – I don't want to see Jack, and I felt sure that Mother will have told Mrs Brigham about me and the mill girls. But Mrs B is so kind. And I needn't have worried about Jack. Neither he nor Mr B came in while we were there. Father is nowhere to be found – again.

Tuesday 2 August

It is a month now since I went to the hospital and the poultice and physic Mrs Legg made for Annie still sit on the bedroom windowsill. I worry about Annie so much. She has not returned to work and I'm beginning to think she never will. I wish I could find out how she is but I don't think Mother will let me go back to the hospital. Am still in deepest disgrace, and not allowed out of the court except to go to work.

Grandfather says I should talk to Mother about Annie. He says he's sure she'll understand. I can't imagine what I'd have done without Grandfather – he's been such a comfort to me. But I do *not* think he's right this time.

Wednesday 3 August

Spoke to Mother about Annie and we will visit her tomorrow. Grandfather is so wise!

Thursday 4 August

Mother and I went to the hospital today but Matron told us that Annie'd been discharged. I didn't believe her – I don't think she even knew who we were talking about! I asked if we could speak to the surgeon. Matron said no at first, but Mother gave her one of her looks and, muttering to herself, Matron went off to find him. She came back a while later and said yes, Annie'd been discharged and that her sister had come for her. But I still didn't think she knew who we were talking about. Don't believe she'd even bothered to find the surgeon.

We went to Annie's court. I was shocked when we got to the entrance. It's awful! So narrow that if I'd stretched out my arm I could have touched the door of the house opposite. Heaps of rubbish everywhere – children playing in it too. They were so ragged and dirty, and they just stared at us with sullen faces when I asked where Annie was. Then suddenly we heard this big snort and we both jumped as this great fat pig waddled round, its snout rootling through the rubbish. When I looked at Mother's face I saw that she was almost as distressed as me.

No one came when I knocked on Annie's door, but at last a woman put her head out of a window and said that Annie and her sister had gone away. She couldn't tell us where – just shrugged and pulled down the window with a bang. I'd been trying not to cry, but at that I burst into tears. Mother put her arm round me and told me that I mustn't worry. That Annie has a sister to care for her. I cried still harder then. I feel as if I abandoned my friend when she most needed help. I don't think I'll ever forgive myself for that.

Friday 5 August

Mrs Elias has been robbed! Some men set upon her in Great Ancoats Street and stole her basket and the little money she had in her pocket. She's an old busybody, that Mrs Elias, and I don't like her, but I felt so sorry when I saw her being helped back into the court. Father's face was grim when Mother told him what had happened. He didn't sound surprised, mind. He said that he'd heard of many such incidents in the last few days.

"The town is very disturbed," he said. "I fear that the police will not be able to keep the peace much longer." The Eliases are poor like us – poorer I think, if what Jack says is true and the wages all spent at the beerhouse. That is what's shocked us so much. It seems that even the poor are turning against the poor now. Father told us we must not go out alone and never after dark. "Promise me, Eliza," he said, looking at me seriously. I gave him my word but felt sore to think that he needed such a promise from me...

Saturday 6 August

The weather is hot and sultry and the heat in that carding room is unbearable. Everyone is snappy and cross – Mr Davis most of all. But today, after my work was done, I braved his temper and nervously asked if he'd had any news of Annie. He looked at me as if he scarcely knew who I was. "No," he said. "But I can tell you that she won't be returning to work here."

Am beginning to feel that I'll never see Annie again.

Monday 8 August

Rumours were flying all around the mill today. All morning I'd done my best to shut my ears to them but as soon as the dinner bell went Biddy and Sarah grabbed my arm and pulled me into the yard. I didn't want to hear what they were trying to tell me, but on and on they went, me hoping and hoping they were wrong. They said that a great strike has begun in the towns to the east of Manchester. Not only mill workers, but miners and labourers, mechanics, carpenters and blacksmiths are throwing down their tools and joining the striking mill hands. They said that the strikers are drawing the plugs from the boilers to stop the steam engines from running and the mills from working. And it all began at a mill in Stalybridge.

I told them I didn't believe them. "It's true," Biddy said. "The hands at Bayley's mill in Stalybridge turned down the wage the master offered. Too low they said it was. Sick of clemming they are."

"And so they pulled the plug from the boiler and marched out!" added Sarah, eyes shining. "They say they'll not go back until they're paid what they got in 1840. Now the hands at many other mills have joined them. Thousands have left their jobs."

I still don't know whether to believe them. How can Biddy and Sarah know what's happening over in Stalybridge?

Mr Davis was nervous and snappy all day. Those rumours must have reached his ears too. Me, I just kept my head down and tried not to think about what was happening so near to us. But deep down I feel sure the rumours are right and a strike *has* begun.

And I can't think of another reason for Father's peculiar cheerfulness as we walked home this evening. Usually he's full of sighs as we walk past the soup kitchens, seeing those hollow faces and scrawny hands clutching tickets for a bowl of soup. But today he was smiling to himself. Actually smiling! And when I asked him what was on his mind he said he felt certain we'd not have to put up with that sight much longer. That soon the masters would see sense and put up our wages. "And then, Eliza," he said, "you will be able to leave the mill…"

But I remember full well the last time a strike was called. We were so short of money and often hungry. Sometimes I fancy I see us standing in that long queue – just as hollow-faced and sunken-eyed as those poor folk we walk past each day. And when I think of the posters plastered all round the town, the thousands filling the streets at that Chartist meeting, I feel sure that this will be a strike like no other we've known.

Tuesday 9 August

The strike has begun! This morning the strikers from Ashton and Stalybridge (almost 10,000 from Stalybridge alone some say!) and all the towns to the east of Manchester poured into the town. Before the dinner bell had gone our engine was stopped and we were all turned out.

I have never been so frightened before. Never! Even now as I write I feel as though I can still hear the shouts and screams in Great Ancoats Street. I don't know which frightened me more – the desperation and anger in the faces of the strikers, or that look in the eyes of the dragoons. They didn't seem to see us as people at all. We were just animals to be cut down. Don't think I'll ever dare set foot out of the house again.

All morning, Mr Davis had looked very agitated. He urged us to keep to our work but then I saw him nip smartly to the window and look out. "Carry on with your tasks," he said, and hurried from the room. Suddenly there was a great crash as the mill gate fell inwards and I jumped with fright. The strikers were pouring into the yard now and I could hear cries and shouts outside our window. Next thing, I heard the glass splinter and looked down to see this big stone lying on the floor. I was shaking all over by now and one or two of the younger hands began to cry. I longed to crawl behind the great machine and hide my head in my arms until it was all over. Then all the machines suddenly stopped, and heedless of the oily floor we flopped down behind them. Mr Davis returned to the room. His face was pale and I could see that he was sweating. "The engine will restart very soon," he said. "A technical hitch. We will all remain here until it does."

Biddy snorted as though she didn't believe him. Somewhere, a long way away it seemed, I heard Mr Davis urge us to stand, but I could not have moved even if I'd wanted to, I felt as if I was stuck to the floor. I could tell from the nearness of the noise that the yard was now full of people. A brick smashed through the window this time, making us scream, and I saw faces pressed up near it. "Come out and join us, fellow hands," a voice cried. "We mean you no harm."

"A fair day's wage for a fair day's labour," cried another. "That's all we want."

We all looked at one another. Mr Davis was

bleating, "Only think ... the danger ... those ruffians..."

His voice was drowned out as the door burst open and I found myself surrounded by other hands.

"Eliza!" called a voice from amongst them. It was Father. Oh, the relief to see him!

"Come," he told me. "I'll take you home. You mustn't stay here."

The room was swarming with people now and Father grasped my hand and told me to hold on tight. "Whatever you do, don't let go," he warned. I felt myself being pulled out of the room. Out of the corner of my eye I could see Mr Davis pinned up against the wall by a couple of men. Out in the yard, we were pulled along by the great mass of people. There were thousands – not just men, but women too. I can't begin to describe what it was like. I was so scared, but I felt oddly excited. Some of the strikers looked so angry, and were carrying big sticks and bricks, but others were smiling – some even singing. Suddenly I found myself wanting to be part of what was happening. But as we left the yard, we were swept up and along Great Ancoats Street by a great heaving mass of people and I felt scared again. Father shouted above the din that he'd try and take me home, but we were forced on, away from the mill and further still from home.

I felt as if I'd suffocate, I could hardly breathe, and then we stopped so suddenly that I was flung forward and almost winded by the people pressed up against my back. I couldn't see anything of what was happening, but I could hear shouts and calls, and then a great hurrah and a big crash as though something large and heavy had fallen. Another great cheer went up, and again I felt myself being pulled forward, along into the yard of a mill over the iron gates now lying on the ground. High above me I saw the last tiny wisps of smoke curl upwards and vanish. Then Father's hand was tugged out of mine. "Father!" I screamed, but he'd disappeared, sucked away from me deep into the crowd.

In vain I tried to force my way back out of the crowd after him. And then, just as I thought I could stand no more, we came to a sudden stop. I stood on tiptoe and could see that we were outside a shop. The shutters were down, but I saw a frightened face appear at an upper window. Then a battering on the door began, and cheers as loaves of bread were tossed at the crowd. I was very hungry and tried to grab some pieces that fell near me, but my arm was pushed roughly away and I had to watch as they were seized and swallowed by a woman standing next to me. I looked at her as she ate, tearing the bread into pieces, muttering and stuffing them into her mouth like a wild animal. It was terrible, that look on her face. As if she hadn't eaten for days.

Scarcely knowing what I was doing, I dived low and tried to crawl out between people's legs. I knew I had to get away. And then I felt a hand reach down and pull me up, and I cried out as fingers dug deep into my shoulder. A voice whispered to me to stop or he'd not answer for the consequences. "Those not with us are against us," he said fiercely. Terrified, I let myself be half-pulled, half-dragged along. I was crying now, my head throbbing with the din. Then, rounding the corner I saw them – a flash of scarlet and gold and chestnut. In my ears now the jangle of the horses' harnesses. As the dragoons neared the mill, I heard a shouted command and with one swift movement, swords sliced through the air.

There were so many of them. So close now that I could see their eyes – and I wanted to cry out to them to stop. I couldn't think why they'd want to hurt me. The hand had let go of my shoulder and I flung myself aside just in time, and now I could hear screams as the strikers turned and saw the dragoons. Pieces of brick were still flying through the air but the crowd had parted now, and those at the back were pushing and shoving to get away from the rearing hoofs.

Strangely, amongst all those screams and shouts I thought I heard faint sounds of hand-clapping – as if orders were being given, but I didn't stop to find out why or what. I turned and ran, back through the fleeing strikers. All the shops had closed, but I could see people peering fearfully out of their windows.

My hand held to my side, I was half running now, half dragging myself along, tripping in my clogs, but I didn't stop until I collapsed against the door of our house.

I think I must have fainted then, because I opened my eyes to find myself on the settle by the fire and Mother staring white-faced at me. Emmy was there and Grandfather too but I couldn't see Father. Emmy burst into tears and I managed a small smile, and then Mother held some water to my lips and I drank and drank.

"Are you hurt?" Mother asked anxiously. Only then did I look down at myself. I was a sight! Covered with dirt, my apron torn, but I was so glad to be home that I hardly cared. I shook my head. And then I asked where Father was.

"Your father has gone out to find you," Mother said tightly. "When he lost sight of you, he came straight here and then went straight back out again." I felt myself tremble and Mother hushed me and hugged me close, rocking me to and fro as if I were Emmy, my head pressed to her shoulder.

Emmy put some water to heat on the fire and then I washed and I heard Mother exclaim as she saw my shoulder. It's black and blue. She sent me upstairs, and I think I fell asleep straight away before I'd even drunk the tea she'd made, because when I woke it was dark and the house quiet, and I have no idea at all how I managed to see to write all this down.

Wednesday 10 August

Father was home when I came down this morning. He looked so tired, great inky smudges under his eyes. I rushed up to him and he hugged me tight. I didn't say anything, just clung to him. Mr Brigham is safe, he told us, but there's still no news of Jack.

I'd not known about Jack being missing. I'd not even thought to ask where he was when I got home yesterday! And when I think of the strikers, and the soldiers galloping around town after them, I feel so afraid for him. Mr Brigham has gone out again to try and find him – oh, please let him be safe!

The whole town has gone mad. Shops looted, their windows smashed. Armed forces patrolling the town, trying to keep the peace. The Ashton and Stalybridge strikers who attacked our mill yesterday have returned home, but at mill after mill the plugs are being drawn, the steam engines stopped and the hands turned out. But many mills do *not* want to join the strike. At one, the hands set a force-pump to work, to throw water on the strikers. But they wouldn't leave – even when some of the hands climbed up on to the roof and began to throw stones and lumps of iron down at them. Several in the yard below were badly hurt, and it's thought a girl may have been killed. But even then, the strikers didn't give up. They seized a cart of coals and began to hurl lumps at the hands. Only when the dragoons arrived did the violence cease and the strikers flee.

"What vandals," said Mother in disgust. Father shook his head. "It's not right. We will never achieve our aims by such acts of violence."

"I am glad to hear that you think so," said Mother tartly.

What about the soldiers! I wanted to shout. I began to cry again as I remembered how they'd plunged among the frightened strikers, hitting out with the flats of their swords. Mother told Father bitterly that it was all his fault and that he should take better care of us. She said that the Chartists were behaving just like the rabble she'd always thought they were. Father was silent – and then he said that the strike had begun out of people's desperation and hunger. The Chartists could not be held responsible for that.

"If the masters had not pushed people so far, none of this would have happened," Father said angrily. "All any of us want is to be paid a decent wage."

"A decent wage," said Mother. "I doubt there'll be any wages, decent or otherwise, coming into this house until this strike is done."

Mrs Elias and Mrs Brigham came round this afternoon. Father was out and Mother still simmering, but she calmed down when she saw Mrs Brigham's face. She looks so tired, as if she's not slept all night. Mrs Elias's black eyes were nearly popping out of her head with excitement. The city is swarming with soldiers, she told us, all armed with swords and rifles. I longed for her to stop, for Mrs B's face had gone as white as chalk. Michael and Emmy jumped up and down with excitement. "We want to go and see the soldiers," they cried.

"You will do no such thing," Mother told them firmly. "You will not leave this court until we tell you it is safe."

Father came home later, a crumpled piece of paper in his hand. It says that all respectable people have been asked to attend the Town Hall to be sworn in as special constables.

"If they want to set worker against worker, this is the best way to do it," he said angrily. He shoved the piece of paper into the fire and was still poking it vigorously long after it had crumbled into ash. As I looked at it, it seemed to me that far more than a piece of paper was burning. Our town, our very lives seem to be crumbling round us.

There's still no news of Jack. Mr Brigham has been to the hospital twice but he's not there. I am glad that he is not lying in bed injured, but I pray the truth isn't worse. I pray he's not lying in some dark cell or even injured by the roadside.

It is late but I couldn't wait for morning to write my news. Jack is home! He has been hurt but he's all right. We all rushed straight next door when we heard he was back. Little Michael was bouncing up and down saying, "Show them where the dragoon cut you, Jack!" We were horrified, but Jack laughed and showed us the graze to his cheek and cuts on his arm. "Just flesh wounds," he said. "I got in the way of a striker's stick. That's all. Not a dragoon's sword, though there were plenty of them around." He told us that he'd been to the infirmary to get his arm dressed, but had discharged himself.

It was good to hear him laugh. I'd hung back at first, for we've not spoken since our quarrel, but he smiled at me so warmly and asked if I was all right and I felt that our differences were all forgotten. He told me he'd been to a meeting at Granby Row Fields. "There were thousands there, Eliza. Many were Chartists of course, but many more were people who just want a fair day's wage for their labour. And we will not return to work until we have it – until the Charter becomes the law of the land. Oh, Eliza, if you could have been there. If you could have heard those words." Dreamily he said: "Better for them to die on the highway, under the pure sun and pure atmosphere of heaven, than to die in the factory attending to machinery. Better to die on the street than surrounded by the rattle box, the thunderous clattering of the machinery and the capitalist."

I didn't like all this talk of dying and I told him so. He laughed. "The men of Stalybridge have a banner," he said. "It says: 'The men of Stalybridge follow wherever danger points the way. They that perish by the sword are better than they that die of hunger.' "

I was beginning to feel frightened and I begged him to stay out of it but I don't think he even heard me. "We must struggle for our rights," he told me. "Together, Eliza."

I felt so scared when I saw the look in his eyes. He seemed to be in a dream and I wanted to shake him out of it. I told him that special constables have been appointed from among ordinary townsmen to break up the riots. That it was dangerous to attend these meetings. But even then I fear I did not wake him.

"Those above us will never do anything for us. The time has come to take matters into our own hands," he said. "And now at last the flame has been kindled. And it is growing. Already it's spreading through Lancashire and Yorkshire. Northwards too. It'll go south and west next – you watch!"

I'm lying here now thinking about that flame. Jack's words sounded so fine but when I remember those strikers rampaging about the town and the look in those soldiers' eyes as they charged, I fear the fire is burning out of control. Who knows where it will end or how it will be put out.

Thursday 11 August

Another Chartist meeting held at Granby Row Fields today. I know because I was there. But I think that my body will remember it long after my mind has forgotten! It isn't just my shoulder that's throbbing now. And it is all Jack Brigham's fault!

I'd not been able to sleep last night – I was tossing and turning so much it was a wonder Emmy didn't wake and clout me one. At about four I got up. I thought I'd heard a sound outside – like a door opening and shutting. I went to the window and looked out. I was right. There was Jack Brigham tiptoeing quickly down the court, his clogs in his hands. I felt sure he was going to another Chartist meeting. He hadn't listened to a word I'd said! I pulled on my clothes and crept out of the house, terror filling my mouth every time I heard the floorboards creak. I had to find him, had to bring him back. I quite forgot the throb in my shoulder, even the fear I'd felt yesterday. Didn't stop to think what Mother would think when she called us for breakfast and found me gone. I didn't dare put on my clogs until I was well out of the court. It was horrid, walking barefoot among all the heaps of muck. I turned into Great Ancoats Street – already full of people, though it was still so early. There were soldiers patrolling the streets, and when I saw them I nearly turned and fled back home, but my worry for Jack was stronger than my fear, and I carried on.

I still couldn't see him but I could see the heaps of stones piled high at street corners, see people scoop them up, hear the smashing of windows. I shut my eyes and ears to all of it. I told myself that I would not go back until I'd found Jack.

Granby Row Fields was packed. I'd been stupid to think I had a hope of finding him. But now that I was there I was not about to run off home. I stood and watched as speaker after speaker climbed up on to a rickety wagon and denounced the masters, telling us not to return to work until our demands were met and the Charter became the law of the land. It had begun to rain now but I could not tear myself away. I scarcely noticed the wet dripping off my hair. I could see that the crowd was peaceful, and I felt sure what the speakers were saying was good and true. The masters will have to listen to us now, I thought, feeling proud and happy. And then I saw men on horseback galloping up to the wagon.

One of them had a piece of paper in his hand and was waving it above his head. I just heard his voice faint and high above the rain. "This meeting is against the law!" he shouted. "It must be stopped." I felt angry then. What right had he to stop a peaceful gathering like this? How could it be wrong? I felt a stir in the crowd, faint, like a tiny shudder of fear. The horsemen had not come alone. Behind them rode three troops of dragoons and a company of soldiers on foot, armed with rifles.

From the wagon the speaker turned to us and, cupping his mouth with his hands, shouted that we must leave now, peacefully, before the Riot Act was read. He said that the town authorities would like nothing better than to see such an outrage as it would give them an opportunity of arresting him.

The Riot Act *was* read then, but I scarcely heard what it said. I couldn't take my eyes off those soldiers.

They had not moved, but all the people around me were beginning to scream and hit out, trying to escape. "What's happened?" I cried to no one in particular.

"Didn't you see the artillery? Run, run now while you can," someone called back. Only then did I see the wagons of the artillery draw up and the soldiers run to their positions near the canal. I tried to run – as far from them as I could, but I felt as though I running round and round in circles. The field was filled with soldiers, and I saw the light glint on their swords as they dashed amongst us.

And then I saw Bob Wavenshawe. Not amongst the screaming men and women, but standing with the other special constables at the exit from the field I was running towards. For a moment I thought I was going mad. But it *was* him, I knew it. I knew that horrible smile. His eyes were fixed on a group of boys just ahead of me.

I heard the lads taunt the constables, and one picked up a stick and held it over his head. "No," another cried, seizing the lad's arm and trying to twist the stick out of it. "All who take part in violence are enemies to freedom, to the Charter." It was Jack.

I screamed at him to run as the constables moved forward, truncheons held high.

Jack turned and saw me and it was that I think that saved him. As he grabbed my arm and pulled me away I saw the constables laying about them with truncheons. I prayed Bob Wavenshawe hadn't seen him. As we hurried away, I saw the lads being rounded up, and the constables march them off the fields.

I told Jack that I'd seen Bob amongst the constables. "Are you sure?" he said. I nodded and saw how angry he looked. Then he told me how stupid *I'd* been! Me! That I should keep away from these meetings! I told him that if I'd not been there it would have been him being marched off to the lock-up! I stalked ahead and wouldn't say another word until we got home.

Mother was up when I got back. I saw her face peering through the window before I reached the door, and she had it open and me yanked inside so fast. The terror I'd seen on her face vanished, I saw her hands clench tightly in her apron and knew I was for it. Father was with her. As he stepped towards me I gasped out Bob's name and they fell silent and looked at each other. "He'll take your job," Mother said bitterly to Father.

Father said he was no better than a knobstick, a strike breaker. He was so angry. But if I'd hoped he'd forgotten me, I was mistaken. Father said he'd just go to the Brighams "to talk some sense into that lad" and then he'd be back to deal with me. I've not heard that anyone was badly hurt in Granby Row Fields today. But *I'll* have to sleep on my stomach tonight.

Friday 12 August

I am in disgrace again and eat my meals alone in my room. Mind, I'm glad to have a little time to myself. I still don't know what to think about the strike. Was it begun by the Chartists? Did they light that little flame? Or was hunger and despair the torch that has set our town alight? I do not know. It's useless to talk to Mother about it. She still says that the strikers are all a Chartist rabble, but I know now it's not that simple. The strikers I saw at Granby Row Fields were peaceful. All they wanted was food for their families and a wage to pay for it. I can't speak to Father either for he's never home. Out at meetings, Mother says whenever I ask. Trying to undo the harm he's started, she says. As if he alone started this strike! As I lie here on my stomach I find myself thinking about William and wondering what he would have made of it all. I cannot tell you, but one thing I do know. He would have been on Jack's side.

Saturday 13 August

Allowed downstairs today, but after Mrs Brigham had come by with her news, I almost wished I wasn't. She says that rioters have tried to break into the gas works to shut down the town's power supply. Now the works are being guarded from further attack by a troop of soldiers and police. And Newton Street police station has been attacked! The mob forced their way in and threw out everything they could find into the street – beds, clothes, pots and pans. Even locks were torn off doors and the front doors of the oven thrown into the street. There were children amongst the rioters too, Mrs B said sadly. When the police arrived, armed with cutlasses, they found one poor policeman cowering under the cellar steps. Nothing remains, only the walls and floors. It is utterly wrecked. I felt myself shiver. "Where will it all end?" I heard Mother murmur. After the door had shut behind Mrs B, I don't think one of us opened it again for the rest of the day.

Sunday 14 August

The government has ordered a fresh troop of soldiers to come to Manchester to help keep the peace. They arrived early this morning by train from London and marched across the town to their barracks in Salford. They have brought fresh artillery with them, Father says, and more troops are expected soon from Ireland. "Even peaceful gatherings are being broken up by the dragoons," he said sadly.

Porridge and watery milk for breakfast. Potatoes again for dinner. But not enough. Emmy keeps whining about how hungry she is and I long for her to stop. The word is now that we are in the grip of a revolution. That the strikes are spreading through the

North country and still further afield. I remember Jack's words about that flame. That flame has spread north into Scotland and now west too into the collieries of Wales. But how can you fight a revolution on an empty stomach?

Monday 15 August

Jack came round to see me this morning. I still feel angry with him and blamed him for my back, which aches when I roll on to it at night. He grinned and said that his dignity hurt more, and that as soon as he was able, he'd bring me what news he could. This afternoon he told me that the streets are quieter, and some of the shops have opened up again. I said I already knew – Mother had gone to the pawnbroker's. Jack was silent for a minute. "I know," he said at last. "My mother went with her…"

Bad news for the strikers pours in. A proclamation has been issued forbidding people to demonstrate or meet together. Even peaceful gatherings are thought to be a threat to the public peace. That proclamation has been signed by the Queen herself, so the strikers must pay heed to that.

Worse news still this evening. Father says that copies of a handbill have been distributed around the town. A £50 reward and a free pardon is promised to anyone who can lay hands on any person who has taken part in the riots, he says. Fifty pounds! That is an enormous sum! I could hardly catch my breath when he told us. Father is sunk in gloom. "The strike will be broken now," he said. "How can a starving man withstand such temptation? He'll betray his own brother for less." Already, he says, people are disappearing and going into hiding for fear of betrayal. Father's words have filled me with such terror. What if Bob *did* see Jack at Granby Row Fields? Will he be able to resist £50? Jack has done nothing wrong, but it'll be Jack's word against that of a special constable.

Tuesday 16 August

Jack's disappeared. Mrs Brigham is beside herself with worry. None of us know what has happened to him. He is not in the infirmary and John Brigham has gone out again to try and find him. I heard him mutter that Jack will feel the back of his hand when he catches up with him. Father looked questioningly at me when he came in and I felt my cheeks redden. But this time I do not know where Jack is and told him so.

Father lost sight of him amongst the crowds that have come to Manchester to celebrate the anniversary of Peterloo. He said the streets were full of people – thousands there were, come from many miles away to see the great procession that was to draw Fergus O'Connor across the town. The procession was cancelled early today for fear the authorities would seize the opportunity to arrest the Chartist leaders. But it was a long time before the news reached the crowds and the streets are still full. Has Jack been seized by Bob Wavenshawe? Has he been arrested and is he now awaiting trial in a prison cell?

Wednesday 17 August

As I sit writing my diary, I look up at the slender tower of the mill chimney. Without the billowing smoke, the sky over Manchester has never looked so clear. The great clattering, thundering, hissing monsters are still. But for how much longer?

Today we heard that a man fired a blunderbuss at some boys to stop them breaking into a print works in Salford. Reports have come that great pieces of railway track have been torn up to stop trains from leaving or entering Manchester at Oldham Road. Sometimes it's hard to know which reports to believe, especially as Mrs Elias is the source of many of them. This afternoon she told us that gangs of youths are roaming the town, setting upon passers-by and breaking the windows of shops. I don't think this report can be true, for she'd *never* venture out of the court if it were.

We're told that the Chartist leaders have imprisoned the town authorities and seized control of the town. That all the Chartist leaders have been arrested and sent to the New Bailey prison. Also that rioters have set upon and murdered the mayor and all the town magistrates. With each day that passes the stories get still wilder. And stuck here at home it's impossible to know what to believe.

This evening there's still no news of Jack and we feel sick with worry. But we've learned that he's not been arrested. I feel sure now that he's gone into hiding. I feel so angry when I think of the worry and trouble he's caused us all.

Thursday 18 August

The spinners, weavers and other trades have been spending much time at Carpenters' Hall, thrashing out ways to end the present "alarming crisis" as Father calls it. There's a plan afoot to send a deputation to the masters to state our grievances. But they have also pledged not to return to work until the People's Charter becomes the law of the land. Will the masters ever agree to our returning to work on such terms? And will the Charter ever become law? I think we'll all have starved before that day comes.

Sunday 21 August

Jack's home at last. Mr Brigham was in such a rage when he returned – the whole court shook with his anger. Down at the end I saw Mrs Elias's window pulled up so that she could have a better listen. Mother pulled ours down quick and I saw how set her face was when she turned round. My legs were shaking, and even Emmy went quiet when she heard those shouts from next door. Bob Wavenshawe has not been here, but it's not just Bob that we have to watch for now. As Father said, we don't know who to trust. And now the Joneses have disappeared. Only been here a short time – but gone already. Flit in the night, Mother says. The house is empty – every stick of furniture gone. Is it poverty or fear that has made them flee? Aren't we even safe in our own court?

Monday 22 August

Mother has found enough money to pay the rent that falls due today, but bit by bit our possessions are finding their way into the pawnbroker's hands. Our dresser's nearly empty now, and the clock gone from the mantelpiece. Mother says tartly that we have no need of it. If this goes on I do not see how we'll be able to hold out. But the hands at our mill say they'll not return until the master puts up our wages and the Charter becomes the law of the land. And the master is as stubborn as his men and will not listen to their demands.

Thursday 25 August

This morning I went round to see Jack. I've not seen him since he returned because I've been feeling so angry with him. But if truth be told, I have missed him too. He's still my friend, I've not forgotten that.

I found him in the cellar making a home for Mrs Legg, Jack's bits of scrap stored away in boxes stacked up by the wall. He told me that Mrs Legg can't afford even the tiny rent for her cellar home. Mrs Legg scrapes a living by taking in washing, delivering bundles to the pawnbroker and minding children. Often she's paid in kind for her simples and poultices. A slice or two of bacon perhaps, or some coals for her fire. But in times like these, families have no money to spare for even these small services. I can't imagine how she's been living and feel such guilt that I'd not thought to ask. Jack says they found her huddled on some dirty straw and shavings – she's even had to pawn her blanket, he says. At least *we* still have beds and blankets and something to sit on. Jack has given her the blanket off the bed he shares with Michael. It'll be more comfortable for her than just straw, he said lightly, but when he said that I felt bad again. I said I'd help him get the cellar clean, and together we swept and washed down the room and then Grandfather, me, Jack and Mrs Brigham helped Mrs Legg move her belongings into her new home. We nailed bunches of dried herbs into the walls and ceiling and arranged her poultices and simples over the fire where the room is driest. Mrs Legg has so little, and without Jack's boxes the room would look very bare.

Tuesday 30 August

The sultry weather frays our tempers, and I get out of the house as often as I can. It's bad now, the smell in our court, but not as bad as the atmosphere at home. This afternoon I sat outside on the step and watched Jack as he worked, his face furrowed with concentration as he hammered at a piece of metal. Some sheets of paper lay next to him and every so often he picked one up and consulted it. I looked at them curiously but the figures and diagrams meant nothing to me. Jack spends most of his time working at his inventions now. He doesn't mention the Chartists, or even the strike. I've never known him so quiet. He seems far away and that makes *me* feel so alone. I do miss my friend.

Tuesday 6 September

Mother and Father fight daily now. I wish they'd stop. Today, as Mother slammed the pot of porridge down on the table, she said she's tired of scraping by. "Can you not find some work to do?" she said despairingly. "I don't care what. Surely there is work to be had cleaning the streets or on the roads?" But Father's so stubborn. He will not break the strike he says. Our best hope is to stand united. Hunger gnaws at my stomach. Sometimes I can think of little else but that.

Wednesday 7 September

This evening I went to visit Mrs Legg. It's stifling hot in that cellar – so hot that I could scarcely catch my breath – but Mrs Legg says that old people feel the cold more and the heat doesn't trouble her much.

When I came to go, she hobbled over to the window and pulled some dry leaves off one of the bunches lying on the sill. I watched as she wrapped them in a twist of paper. "You're looking pinched, lass," she said, handing it to me. "They'll do for your tea." I thanked her but when I got home I hid them in my diary. I could just imagine the look on Mother's face if I tried to boil those leaves up for tea! But we could all have done with something to take away the taste of that pie Mother made for our dinner. At least that was what she called it, but to me it was just a mess made of flour, oatmeal and water. More floury water than oatmeal I think. It was so disgusting that my empty stomach heaved and Emmy was actually sick. Father tried to cheer Mother by saying that with a bit of pickle that pie would make a fine meal. He even finished his plateful – just to please her I think. Anyway, when we sat down for tea this evening, there were potatoes on the table again. Half each, and a bit extra for Father. I don't know where they came from, but I was glad to see them!

Thursday 8 September

There's one thing I'm grateful for – the house does not get so dirty now that so few mills are working, and anyway, there's little enough furniture left to wipe down. This has been making Mother cross, but she *is* much more cheerful today. She believes that the strike will soon be over and that Father and I will be able to return to work.

And I am heartily sick and tired of meal porridge and oatcakes. Sick, sick, sick! And when Mother pours out the tea it is a strange colour – a sort of grey from the tea leaves being used so often. When I think of these things I long for the strike to end. Then I remember the carding room, the fluff that filled my chest and stomach. Though I am always hungry, I dread the day I must walk back into that place.

Saturday 10 September

Today we learned that the hands at our mill have given in. The master has won. We return to work on Monday. I feel such a sinking in the pit of my stomach and it does not go away even when I tell myself that at least we'll soon be able to fill our bellies again.

Monday 12 September

Back at work. Went with dragging feet and heavy heart. Most of the Manchester mills are already back at work, yet the soup kitchens are still open and the streets as full of people as before. People with no jobs to go to and nothing to fill their bellies. Nothing has changed. We are back where we were when the strike began. Our wages have not been put up, and the Chartists' plan for a general strike to follow the shutting of the mills has failed. Father didn't say a word to me as we made the short walk from home to the mill. But the bitterness I see in his face tells me that he's as heavy-hearted as I am. I remember Jack's words and feel some of that bitterness too. The great flame that fanned across the North country has been put out at last.

Wednesday 14 September

Two of the spinners have been dismissed for their part in the strike and their big piecers have been given their wheels! Father said angrily that they weren't even given the opportunity to explain themselves, just told to leave immediately. He knows the men well and can vouch for their upright conduct.

When the bell rang for dinner, he went to the master to speak on their behalf. Later I asked him how the master came by his information. "From one of the special constables," he said shortly. "A most respectable and public-spirited man," he added ironically. I thought of Bob Wavenshawe then and I felt all shivery inside. What if Bob learns that Father also supported the Chartists? Bob would see it as his duty to tell the master and his reward would be Father's wheels.

"Please don't speak to the master again," I cried. "No matter who it is or what it's about." He looked at my worried face and promised he would do nothing to put at risk either his job or his family's future. But Father works by Bob's side, day after day. As long as he does that, I don't think any one of us will ever feel truly safe again.

Friday 16 September

Now I have another fear to deal with. I must tell you at once for I feel all chewed up inside with worry. The government has begun to hunt down the Chartists. "Agitators" they're calling them. Hundreds have been thrown into prison and are awaiting trial, so Jack says. I could hardly keep the wobble out of my voice when

I asked Jack if he knew what would happen to them. Prison for some for sure, but, he said, there are rumours that some may even be transported to Australia. Transportation! I know that Father has done nothing wrong, but I can't forget how easily those spinners were dismissed. None of us knows what has happened to them. Are they awaiting trial for their part in the strike? Are any of us safe?

Friday 23 September

Now Fergus O'Connor has been arrested! I wasn't surprised, not now I know how many others have been taken. I heard the news from Jack when I saw him in the yard this evening. He took my arm and pulled me aside, looking round carefully to make sure we were alone. Jack said it happened in London on Wednesday. He says it's for getting people to riot, but I said I thought that the strikes would have happened anyway. People had had enough of going hungry, hadn't they? Jack says that another of the Chartist leaders, Mr M'Douall, has even fled to America to escape arrest. That is a fair way to go, but sometimes I find myself wishing that we could go there too.

Saturday 24 September

Now that Father and I are back at work, that strained look has quite left Mother's face, and this evening I even caught her humming when we got in. It made me want to scream. It was as if everything was back as it should be and I know that it is not. Not for me anyway. Everything is wrong.

Friday 30 September

The Brighams are leaving! Mrs Brigham broke the news to us this evening. I can't begin to tell you how awful I feel. We've all come to depend on them so much. They are going so far away ... to *America*.

Mother was so shocked when Mrs Brigham told her that she dropped the kettle she was holding and it fell to the floor with a heavy clang. None of us made any move to pick it up. She sat down heavily and I went and stood next to her and put my arm round her shoulders. I looked at Jack. He was trying to hide how he felt but I could see in his face how happy he really was. I was feeling as though the bottom had fallen out of my stomach. I looked at Emmy to see how she took the news. She's become great friends with Michael, and I saw how her face puckered up. Mr Brigham told us that they plan to go to Pennsylvania. "The East-coast mills are already flooded with immigrants from England and Ireland looking for work," he said. "But we have learnt that there's work to be had in Pennsylvania." Not just in the mills, he said, but on the land, and on the roads and canals. "The future here is far from certain," said Mr Brigham. "And I want Jack and Michael to have the opportunities they'll never have in England."

For a minute I found myself wishing that I could go too. But America ... such a big place and so far away from all that I know ... I thought of the great ocean dividing Manchester from America and found myself wanting to cry.

Saturday 1 October

After supper this evening we all walked out into Ancoats together. It's so long since we've done this. Helsteds and Brighams together. I'd have felt happier if I'd not had in mind that it was probably the last time. The beerhouses were quieter than usual, but the sound of singing voices and the scraping of fiddles drifted out to us through the windows. The jolly music made me feel sadder still. Jack was silent for a time, walking by my side. There seemed such a gulf stretching between us – as if the great ocean already separated us. At last Jack told me how excited he felt to be going to America. I said nothing and looked at the ground. Jack's foot was kicking at a stone. "I will miss you," he said, and I looked up and saw that his eyes were on the ground too. "Truly I will. I don't want to lose another friend." He looked at me and I saw how sad his face was. "Can you not persuade your father to bring you too?" he said. I shook my head. I told him that Mother'll not even leave our house. "She'll not leave William," I said. "The house holds all that is left of him for her."

"And what do you want?" Jack asked.

"What does it matter what I want?" I said, bleakly.

"It matters," Jack said, with a little of his old fierceness. "Eliza, so long as you live in England, your future will always lie in the hands of the mill owners…"

Sunday 2 October

Jack Brigham came to our door this evening, his hands full of evergreen and wild flowering herbs. Without a word, he thrust them into mine. At first I was surprised and puzzled, I could not think what made him do that. Now I think I know. And for the first time in so long I felt my spirits rise.

Thursday 13 October

Noises coming from next door again. The Brighams are preparing to leave. They go on Sunday. I watched as Jack and Mr Brigham tried to manoeuvre the dresser out of the door and into the street. Piece by piece their furniture has been sold to help pay for their passage. I hate to see it go; it brings home to me how soon they'll be leaving us.

Saturday 15 October

Brighams joined us for supper this evening. Furniture is all sold and everything's packed up ready for their departure in the morning. Mr Brigham has told us that his cousin, Peter Cooke, is planning to take his family to America too. He asked Father whether he had any thought of joining them. I looked at Father

149

but it was in Mother's face that I knew I'd find my answer. I know she will *never* leave this house.

Sunday 16 October

They went today. Actually saw them get on the train and go.

They had to take the train from Manchester to get to Liverpool docks where they board the brig that will take them to New York. Mrs Brigham had wanted us to make our farewells last night. "We'll be up at first light and that girl of yours needs her sleep," she said, smiling and nodding at me. I was about to blurt out that I'd do my catching up later, when Mother interrupted. "It's a fair walk to the railway and you'll need help with all that baggage," she said. I saw her look askance at Jack's invention as she spoke, and Mr Brigham caught that look and burst out laughing. "Jack will leave his head behind before that," he said, nodding at it. From the look on Mother's face it was plain that that was exactly what she thought Jack was doing. Jack shrugged, but didn't say anything. He has such faith in that invention of his. I know he hopes he'll sell it to the master of some works in America.

Mother had her way and in the end we all went to the station with them – even Grandfather, though Mother had wanted him to stay home. He insisted he'd manage and took my arm – I could tell he was keen to see that train.

When we reached the station Jack suddenly turned round to me and pressed a book into my hands. "I hope you'll enjoy it, Eliza," he said shyly. I looked at the little book – *A Curious Herbal* by Elizabeth Blackwell it said on the cover. Inside Jack had written,

To my very dear friend, Eliza, from her friend Jack

All of a sudden I felt choked up again. Without thinking I flung my arms round him and hugged him and hugged him. When at last I let go of him I saw how red his face had gone and I felt mine grow pink too then. "Wish I had something for you," I said at last.

He pointed to all the bags piled around them. "It is as well you didn't," he said. He was trying to smile, but I could see that his eyes were bright. "I will write, Eliza. I promise. Just as soon as we're settled. But please, try and persuade your father to bring you to America. Promise me."

I promised. I could not say much more for my voice was wobbling. And then I heard Jack's father call to him to hurry, for it was time for them to climb on board. It was a bit of a squash when they were all on – all those families and bundles and boxes crammed together. Then I heard a muffled shout and I saw John Brigham fight his way back to the window and beckon to Father. Father climbed up the little wooden steps and I saw Mr B lean out of the window and press a piece of paper into his hand.

"It's the address of our cousins at Bank Top," he said. "Write to them if you change your mind."

A whistle went then and a guard waved to Father to stand away as the train lurched forward – so slowly at first, then faster and faster. Faster than the boats on the canal, faster than a horse-drawn cab or wagon in Great Ancoats Street. I ran down the platform and then stood and watched as the big black train grew smaller and smaller.

Wednesday 26 October

Today I am fourteen. We are so short of money that I was not expecting any presents, but when I got home from the mill there they were laid out on the table for me. Mother has made me a new apron. It is sewed with finer stitches than my clumsy fingers could ever manage. Emmy has made me a handkerchief into which she has stitched my name and the date. I gave her a hug. "It is beautiful," I told her, and I watched her cheeks go rosy with pleasure. Mother would like Emmy to become apprenticed to a dressmaker when she's older but Father says the hours are even longer, the pay worse, and the work harder than at the mill. Father gave me two green ribbons. Chartist green, I thought, suddenly remembering the ribbons the women had worn at the Chartist meeting. I'd forgotten that – how long ago it all seems now. We never mention that time, and with no Jack to talk to I feel strangely removed from it all. For a moment I felt sad again, remembering, and I tied the ribbons into my hair. Father smiled as he watched me and I felt that just this tiny gesture had made him a little happier.

Dear Grandfather! He walked all on his own to Mrs Legg's and brought back a little pot of ointment, which he says will help soothe my aching feet and legs. I rubbed some on when I went up to bed and looked at the herbs and flowers Jack had given me. I'd put them on the windowsill to dry when they'd died but their sweet smell still lingers. The little book he gave me lies next to my precious diary. I miss him so much.

Thursday 27 October

Bob Wavenshawe was in the yard when I left work today. He smiled that wolfish smile of his at me. I just hurried on. I could feel his stare on my back and I walked still faster.

I wish he'd leave the mill. I hate the thought of Father working so closely with a man like that.

Sunday 30 October

Went to Green Heys Fields today in honour of my birthday. I was so excited I thought I'd never be able to sleep, but Mother had to call several times to wake me this morning. I'm finding it hard getting used to mill hours again and I sleep so heavily.

The trees were laden with russet and were glowing gold in the autumn sun. It was still quite warm, and Emmy and I kicked off our heavy wooden clogs to feel the soft springiness of the grass under our feet. We played hide and seek and blind man's buff. Emmy screamed as I pushed her towards Grandfather – he was whirling round in a spin, his arms flailing about him. How we laughed to see him! Mother had packed some food to take with us – buttered oatcakes and, best of all, a slice of gingerbread each! I bit into it. How good it tasted out there in the fresh air. "Food gives heart," said Grandfather smiling at me. But best of all was being happy together – a proper family again.

Tuesday 1 November

Last night was All Hallow's Eve and Grandfather was as full of tales as ever as we sat round the fire. At last Mother told him to watch his tongue or he'd have Emmy up all night with nightmares! But we love to listen to his stories. Of gorges where goblins crouch, and Pendle Hill up north where witches once rode on broomsticks, and Pendle Forest where ghostly horses and hounds were sometimes seen by any folk foolish enough to stop out at dusk. Grandfather says there's not a marsh or blasted tree or ruin anywhere in that wild place that did not once have its own boggart. "But that was long ago," he said, smiling at our terrified faces. "Long long ago, even before I was born. There were no mills then."

It wasn't Emmy but me who couldn't sleep! My mind was full of those stories from another place and time, and in the end I crept downstairs and sat looking into the dying embers of the fire still thinking about them. How I'd love to see the countryside Grandfather once knew so well.

Must have drifted off then for I woke with a jump to feel Mother's hand on my shoulder. It was morning. The fire had gone out and I was frozen.

Friday 4 November

A great fire broke out today at Pooley's mill in Mill Street. We were all shocked, for the fire spread so fast that many of the hands were trapped inside the building. The main staircase was choked with smoke and burning flames and there was no other way the hands on the upper floors could get out. I'd known there'd been a fire before I got home. We'd been able to smell the smoke in the yard when we came out of the mill this evening. Even now as I write, I fancy I can see the flames and I can still smell that smoke. Our court stinks of it. Am so glad that I don't work at Pooley's mill – I don't think I could bear to walk through the gate again knowing that so many of my work mates died there.

Sunday 6 November

Have been reading the little book Jack gave me. It is quite beautiful and today it's helped to take my mind off the thought of the dead at Pooley's mill. On each page is drawn a flower or herb and underneath its name its uses are written. Here are plants to relieve a cough, plants that will ease rheumaticky fingers and numb toothache. I showed the book to Grandfather. His eyes lit up when he saw the pictures. We were so engrossed that we didn't hear Mother call us for tea. Grandfather asked if he could show the book to Mrs Legg, and when the plates were cleared away we went to visit her. While she and Grandfather sat together and turned the pages, I looked round Mrs Legg's new home. It's as neat and clean as her old home ever was – drier than the Brighams' cellar too, I think. Grandfather had brought some kindling for her fire but we were pleased to see that one was already lit and burning in the grate.

Before we left, Mrs Legg took Grandfather's hands in hers and squeezed them in her mottled shaking ones. Her eyes are as bright and black as a robin's. For a long minute I watched as they stood there holding each other's hands. As I looked at her I found myself thinking how frail and thin she's grown. As if the slightest puff of wind would blow her away – back to the countryside where she belongs.

Tuesday 8 November

Took Jack's book with me to work today. It was a dry day but blustery, and as soon as I'd finished cleaning, I wrapped my shawl close round me and joined Sarah in the yard. "What's that?" she said, looking at my book curiously. I showed it to her proudly but after turning over a few pages she handed it back to me without a word and went back to her novelette. Sat awhile with the little book on my lap. It is now nearly a month since we saw the Brighams off at the railway station. I thought of them in a little ship out on the vast ocean and shivered. When I looked up I saw Bob Wavenshawe in the yard again, leaning against the wall and staring at me. I shut the book quickly and went inside.

Friday 11 November

Factory inspector at the mill today. Biddy says that the inspectors can visit a mill without warning the masters first, but from the smirk on Mr Davis's face I felt sure he had been expected. Biddy said later she'd guessed that a factory inspector was in town. I asked her how she knew. "Because our drinking water was changed twice this morning," she said, pulling a face. "Word soon gets around." But that smirk dropped off Mr Davis's face quick enough when the inspector spotted the broken ventilating wheel. We'd just stopped for dinner – on time for once – and the air was cleaner than it is when the machines are running, but the inspector could see the fine white dust on our hair and clothes well enough. He called Mr Davis over and I saw him bow and scrape as he assured the inspector that the wheel would be fixed. I don't know that the inspector was that happy, mind. He kept shaking his head and writing things in his notebook. Then he called us up to him one by one to check our names and ages. Little Mary Whittle looked so frightened when her turn came, and I did not wonder for it's clear to all us hands that she cannot yet be nine. But that was what she told the inspector.

"I'm nine, mister. Promise," she said over and over. I felt so sorry for her! The inspector sighed and told her she could go, but he called Mr Davis over to him again. He was looking so serious; I could tell he didn't believe a word she'd said, and when Mr Davis scuttled over he looked almost as scared as Mary.

Later, Father and I talked about the factory inspector's visit, and I told him how he'd looked into the buckets and at the broken wheel and how he'd checked all our ages. "He found the room dusty as the wheel does not work," I said. "But at least it is not as hot now as it was in the summer." Then I told him about Mary. Father sighed when I'd finished. "I wish you didn't have to work there, Eliza," he said at last. "I wish I knew what best to do for us all." I asked him if he'd had any news of the Brighams. He shook his head. "But don't worry, Eliza," he said. "Even a steamer takes at least two weeks to cross the Atlantic. A sailing brig is very much slower — it may be two months or even longer before they reach New York. And remember: even after they've landed they have a further journey inland to Pennsylvania. I don't think that we'll hear from them for some weeks yet."

Saturday 12 November

There was another child standing in Mary's place this morning. Sarah thought Mary had already been dismissed. But I think she's run away. The look on Mr Davis's face said it all. Such relief! Biddy agreed. "The inspector won't be able to prove her age now," she said. "The master won't have to get rid of her." I asked her what she thought Mary will do now. Biddy shrugged. "She will find a job at another mill where they're not fussy about employing under-age children," she said. I am not as sure as Biddy about that, for there are so few jobs to be had.

But our drinking water has been changed three

times today and the ventilating wheel is to be fixed. Just little things, but they'll make the carding room a better place to work in. They cost the master so little but make such a difference to us.

Saturday 19 November

It's the strangest thing but wherever I go now, I seem to see Bob Wavenshawe. Sometimes I think I'm imagining it but whenever I come out into the mill yard for dinner there he is. And when I leave work, he's there again – even when I'm late. And whenever he catches my eye, he doesn't look away, just carries right on staring at me. Staring and smiling. Now when I leave the mill I try to make sure that one of the other girls is with me. I do not want to be alone with him. Biddy and Sarah say they've noticed how he looks at me. They say it makes their flesh crawl.

After I finished work today there Bob was as usual, lolling near the mill gate, staring at me as hard as ever. Father was with him, mind, and when he saw me he called me over. I walked over ever so slowly, scuffing my feet, wishing that something would happen to make Bob disappear. Father put his arm round me and gave me a hug. Bob smirked. "Your daughter's growing into a fine girl," he said. Father just looked at me proudly and smiled. He didn't see the look Bob gave me I could tell. Father still thinks of me as his little girl. He does not see that I am growing up.

Sunday 27 November

Mrs Legg is dead! I feel so sad to think that I'll never see her again. Grandfather's eyes were red-rimmed when he told us. Mrs Legg wanted him to have all her things. He said she also had a message for me. "Tell the little one that it is through the *young* that the *old* ways live on." Felt so strange when Grandfather said that. I told him I would try, but that I don't really know how. And anyway, if we're to stay in Manchester, how can I do what Mrs Legg wants? Grandfather just smiled and said that somehow we'd find a way.

He wanted to bring Mrs Legg's things here – all of them, even the bundles of herbs and drying plants that used to hang from her ceiling. But Mother would have nothing to do with it. "You will bring disease in to the house," she said. Grandfather said nothing but I could see he was upset and that upset me still more. Mrs Legg's home was always spotless. How could Mother think her few possessions could bring harm to anyone? "Why won't you let Grandfather bring her things here?" I cried. "How can they harm us?"

"I'll not have them in the house," Mother said. "How do we know what killed her? Those bad smells were enough to make anyone ill."

"She made Michael better," I said stubbornly. Mother raised her eyebrows. "Michael is a strong child," she said. "His arm would have got better without anyone's help."

And then I said the words I'd give anything to take back. But you can't take them back. Not words like those. "She'd have helped William too if only you'd let her." That was what I said. I'd spoken quietly but Mother heard, I know full well she did. Not the words, but my meaning – it was clear on my lips and in my eyes. She looked as stricken as if I'd accused her of killing William with her own hands. I felt terrible when I saw her face, but even now, nearly three years after his death, I've not been able to put out of mind how Mother refused to let Mrs Legg help him.

Mother goes about the house looking so hurt. I don't know what to say or do to take that hurt away.

"Your mother did what she thought best for William," Grandfather said. "Remember that. His lungs were bad and he was always frail. He could never have flourished here in Manchester." I am even more determined now that we must get away from Manchester. I feel sure that he is right. Nothing good can grow and flourish here.

Monday 28 November

Helped Mother with the chores this evening though I was tired when I got home. I want to make amends for my words yesterday and I can't think of a better way. As I look at her hands – chapped and raw from washing and cold – I feel so guilty. Jack was right. I have been selfish. I am still a child – like a child I've thought only of my own troubles.

Saturday 17 December

Haven't been keeping up my diary, but then have some excuse for this. Hands are sore with chilblains and it hurts to write much. And anyway, I have so little to write about. Weather is both cold and wet and keeps us indoors a lot of the time. I feel so miserable, stuck inside so much. When I'm not at the mill, I'm imprisoned within the four walls of our house. Mother does not like us to leave the court without either her or Father. I tell her I'm sure it is safe to go out now. But she says that with each week that passes the streets are becoming more dangerous.

Sunday 18 December

Today Father took Emmy and me to Green Heys to pick mistletoe and holly and greenery to decorate the house for Christmas. I cheered up a little as we entered the fields. They looked so beautiful – the trees and grass all white with frost. The pond had frozen too and Emmy and I wanted to slide on it, but Father took a long stick and prodded it to show us how thin the ice still was in the centre. Oh, but it was cold! I had to hop from foot to foot to try and keep warm, and by the time we'd picked all the greenery we needed I could scarcely feel my feet and fingers. We played a game of chase to try and warm ourselves before the long walk home and I bunched up my skirts and slid across the fields, my hair slipping loose under my shawl, my clogs falling off. Emmy slipped and grazed her knee on the icy ground but for once she didn't howl. Just picked herself up and hobbled after me again! She was as pleased as me to be out in the fresh air again.

When we got back we pinned bunches of holly to the walls and over the chimneypiece, and a little bunch of mistletoe over the door. But I do not feel the cheer I usually feel at Christmas. Like many of the houses in Ancoats, the houses of our neighbours stand silent and empty. It is not as Christmas should be.

Christmas is a time for friends and families but *our* friends are so far away.

Friday 23 December

At last a letter has come from the Brighams. They have arrived in Pennsylvania! The crossing was rough. There was too little space for the emigrants, so they had to bunk as best they could, and many people fell sick crammed like cattle as they were below deck. But they arrived without mishap and Mr Brigham and Jack have found work digging a railroad. Jack's still trying to sell his invention and find employment at an engineering or mill works. But at least they are safe. Away from horrible Manchester and best of all, away from the mill and the troubles which face us here. I wonder when I will hear from Jack. I can't help but feel a little annoyed that he has not yet written to me.

Sunday 25 December

A cold wintry day. Mother sent me round to ask the Eliases to join us for dinner but they're going to spend the day with their cousins. Was relieved, though Mother said I should show more charity at Christmas time. For our dinner we had a fine piece of roast pork and then Mother brought in the pudding. Father declared it was the finest he'd ever eaten. Afterwards Father stoked up the fire and we huddled close by it and gave each other our presents. Grandfather quietly slipped me a little package of dried camomile, which I think he must have put by from Mrs Legg's hoard. "Don't tell your mother," he whispered. I wonder how many more of Mrs Legg's ointments and poultices he's hidden away. Before we went to bed, Father toasted "absent friends", which made Mother, me and Emmy cry. Grandfather tried to cheer us by telling us about Christmases he remembered from his childhood. How they brought in the yule log on Christmas Eve and decorated it with evergreens. He said it had to be dragged to the door by a carthorse for it was far too big and heavy to carry. Practically a tree, Grandfather said proudly holding out his arms to show its girth. We all burst out laughing. I thought Father would choke, he was laughing so much! Grandfather grew up in a cottage, as did his father and grandfather before him. Father still remembers it.

Sunday 1 January, 1843

The streets are full of people, all noisily wishing each other a happy New Year. Such relief I see on people's faces as we greet each other in the streets. Everyone is as glad as we are to see the back of 1842. We'd spent New Year's Eve quietly at home, and it was before midnight when we went up to bed. I think we all wanted to hurry out the old year as fast as possible.

Wednesday 4 January

It was late when I left the carding room, for Mr Davis had kept me back to clean as usual. As I came out into the yard there Bob was again. My heart sank to see him still there, right by the gate too where I had to pass him. I looked round for Biddy and Sarah but they'd already gone and I was alone. I tried to hurry past, keeping my eyes to myself, but he came up to me rubbing his hands and I heard the fingers crack. I winced, stepping back quickly, and I saw those lips draw back over the yellow teeth in that wolfish smile. I could see just how pleased he was to have found me alone. He asked if he could walk me home. "The streets are still not safe, Eliza," he said. "You never know who might be there."

I told him politely that Mother did not like me to walk out with men. "Not even with an old friend like me?" he said, smirking and edging closer. I shuddered and quickly pushed past him and ran through the gate. I heard him shout something angrily after me. Fear twisted inside me but I didn't stop running until I got home. Mother was outraged when I told her what had happened.

"I'll tell your father," she said. "He'll speak to him and put a stop to this nonsense."

"No, Mother," I cried, and I told her what Bob had called after me. That he knew about the part Father had played in the strike. That he was a Chartist rabble-rouser. Mother looked at me sharply. "Are you sure?" she said. "It is rubbish. Your father has done nothing wrong." I told her I didn't think that'd make any difference. My voice trembling, I reminded her about the spinners, dismissed so lightly after the strike, about the arrests of Chartists across the country.

"I told him not to get involved with those people," she said bitterly.

And now Father's home I can see the worry as clear in his face as I can in Mother's – for all he says that Bob can't get him dismissed.

Wednesday 11 January

A letter from Jack arrived today! It was waiting for me when I got home and I raced straight upstairs to read it. He's still working on the railroad, still hoping to sell his invention…

"But Mr Smythson of Smythson's mill has expressed interest in it, and I am hopeful that a place will be found for me in his workshop…" he wrote.

I was so excited when I read that! And so proud.

"America is a wonderful place. It is a place where hard work and enterprise are rewarded. Please, Eliza, urge your father to bring you here. Father thinks that his cousin, Peter Cooke, will bring out his family soon…"

They are treated with respect in America, Jack writes. Church ministers, engineers, and even the mill masters see them as equals there, for they were immigrants themselves once. They work alongside Poles, Russians, Germans, as well as Irish and English families. They can't all understand each other, but he's beginning to learn about their lives and the homes they have left. Many of these people have had to flee persecution at home, far worse than anything we have endured. But America opens her arms to all.

Friday 13 January

Another letter arrived today. Two in one week! Father said it's from John Brigham's cousin, Peter Cooke. He writes that they plan to join the Brighams as soon as they can arrange passage to New York. Peter Cooke is a spinner in New Eagley Mill. That's near Turton, a little place to the north of Manchester. At first I couldn't think why Peter Cooke wanted to write to us – and Father wouldn't say, just laughed and hid the letter away. But he looked so thoughtful when he'd finished reading it, and later I saw him write back. He wouldn't tell me what he wrote, mind, but I notice he's not wasted much time in replying. I can't stop thinking about that letter. Has he at last managed to persuade Mother to leave our little court?

Sunday 22 January

Father has gone to meet Peter Cooke. Mother won't say why, but the expression on her face has raised my hopes again. Has Father gone to discuss arrangements for our passage to America? Why else would he go all that way?

I found myself thinking about the Brighams then. I have been sitting awhile with Jack's book in my lap but I cannot concentrate on it at all. My eyes keep turning to the window. It is snowing hard now and Father is still not back.

Monday 23 January

I was so relieved when I saw Father tiptoeing into our room this morning! The snow in the country was deep, Father said, and on his way home, the horse pulling the wagon slipped in a snowdrift and it was only when another wagoner stopped to help that they managed to pull it out again. I asked him why he had gone all that way in the snow.

He hesitated but I begged him to tell me. At last he said he was hoping to take over Peter Cooke's job at New Eagley Mill! "He has no one to leave his wheels to," said Father. "Eliza, I didn't want to tell you just yet. I didn't want to raise false hopes. I have yet to meet Mr Ashworth, the owner of the mill." He smiled at me. I tried to smile back but his words filled me with such bitter disappointment.

The Ashworths' mills are famous for the quality of their yarn, Father said, but even they have had trouble selling it these past months, as the demand for cotton has fallen. Yet the cloth spun and woven at the Ashworths' mills is amongst the finest in England and there is hope that trade will soon pick up. There are two mills, he said – one at nearby Egerton as well as New Eagley. The owners are two brothers – New Eagley is run by the elder, Henry Ashworth.

I had to stop myself from telling Father I didn't care. Instead I said that I'd thought he'd been planning to take us all to America. He seemed surprised. I don't think the idea had even entered his head!

"How could we take your grandfather?" he asked. "He is getting frail now, Eliza. I don't think he would survive such a voyage. And we can't ask him to shift from lodging house to lodging house while we look for work." Also, Mother would never uproot herself from England. But I find it hard to put aside my disappointment. I tell myself that once I could have asked for nothing more. Living in the country has been my dream ever since I was a little girl. But will I just be changing one place of slavery for another? Will I still be a mill girl?

Thursday 2 February

Another letter from Jack! He writes that it is cold and miserable work digging the railroad. But he has a promise of work from Mr Smythson. "By the time you get this letter," he writes, "I will be a mechanic in Smythson's mill." He sounds so proud. I wrote straight back and told him how proud we are of him, but oh, how I wish I could have been there to tell him face to face.

Tuesday 7 February

Father has heard from Mr Ashworth! He's been asked to present himself at New Eagley Mill on Sunday bringing a testimonial from the master. We're all excited. Father most of all I think.

Sunday 12 February

Father returned to New Eagley Mill this morning. He started very early but we all got up to see him off – we were so excited! Mother gave Father a good looking over before he left. She straightened his necktie and smoothed his hair just as if he was a little boy. And Father seemed different somehow. Younger, full of energy. I could see Mother thought so too, for she didn't stop smiling as she looked at him. Now there's nothing we can do but wait. But the waiting's so hard, and when I look at my pencil I see that I have chewed it again. I must try not to. It's nearly down to a stub now and I need to save what's left.

Monday 13 February

Father has got Peter Cooke's job. We are leaving Manchester! We're moving to the country! Today

Father formally gave notice that we'll be leaving our employ in Ancoats in a month's time. "The Ashworths are good masters," he said. "We are very lucky that Peter Cooke has no family here to leave his wheels to. So few jobs like this come up at the Ashworths' mills."

I was so excited at that moment that I rushed over to Grandfather and seized his hands and we smiled and smiled at each other. I thought we'd never stop smiling. How good it will be to get far away from Manchester and that awful Bob Wavenshawe.

Father laughed and even Mother smiled, but it was such a sad little smile. I went over to her and hugged her and she held me tightly against her for a minute. It will be hard for Mother leaving this house. It'll be hard for all of us. This house holds all that is left of William. But I know it's time now to move on, and when Mother laughed and released me it felt as if she knew that too.

Wednesday 15 February

A mill girl I am and a mill girl I remain. Today I was given the answer I'd been dreading. A job's been found for me in the carding room at New Eagley Mill. I'll not be stopping work when we leave Manchester. I'll simply be exchanging one workplace for another.

"The Ashworths' mills are good places to work," Father said once again. "I've seen them for myself. The rooms are airy and clean. The hands are well treated and there's a library where you can borrow books." If he thought that would comfort me, it didn't. I'm still just a pair of hands.

Sunday 19 February

Wrote to Jack with our news today. Father has already sent word to the Brighams.

Too cold to write more.

Wednesday 22 February

After I left the mill today I went to see Miss Croom. She was startled to see me at the door and I wasn't surprised. I haven't once been back to see her since we left school. The memories made it too painful. I tried to explain this and I think she understood. She said she knew that mill work was hard, and few of her scholars found the energy to continue their studies. "Even the clever ones," she said, smiling at me. My face flushed pink when she said that! Then she asked me why I had come to see her now, and I told her that we're leaving Manchester and moving to Eagley. I told her how much I wanted to leave the mill and carry on with my studies but I didn't know if I'd ever be able to.

"There are so few opportunities, Eliza," she said. "Especially for girls. You must seize whatever chances come your way." She told me to make good use of the library at Eagley. But I do not know how I'll find the time or energy for study if I am still to work.

Walked the long way home – down to the canal and past Mr Brown's shop. I skirted round it, but I could see it was boarded up and no sign of Mr Brown. The canal was as black and stinking as ever, but I didn't mind looking at it now, for soon I'll be gazing into the clear waters of Eagley Brook. Then back into Great Ancoats Street. I've always liked it here. Today it looked different somehow. Those little shops – how scruffy and dirty they are. At last I reached the mill – how I hate it. Hate it all!

Saturday 25 February

We don't leave for two more weeks, but already Mother's begun to sort our clothes and possessions. Those clothes that are too worn to be mended are got rid of. Anything we do not really need is sold: the money's to help pay for our journey to Eagley. Father tells her to go steady. "We will need to furnish our new home," he said laughingly.

Our new home is a sore point with Mother. She had thought we'd be moving into Peter Cooke's old home in Bank Top – the village next to New Eagley Mill.

But Father says Mr Ashworth's cottages are only given to those who've proved their loyalty over many years' service. Mother's convinced that Father is taking us to live in a rickety cottage far from the village. Worst of all, maybe even in nearby Bolton. But Father says he's found us a snug little cottage to live in. With a garden of our very own! Felt so excited when he said that! Grandfather and I spent the rest of the evening planning all the flowers and herbs we'll grow in it.

Saturday 4 March

There are a few things Mother will not get rid of. While she thinks I'm not looking, I see her pack a few of William's things into one of the boxes. It's as if by this she's able to take William with us. She will not – she cannot – leave anything of him behind.

One more week.

Sunday 12 March

We're here at last – at Peter Cooke's home. Crept out of bed to write my diary in the moonlight. It was a bit of a struggle, mind, because there are four of us in the bed – Emmy, me, and Jenny and Harriet, the two Cooke girls. We lie top to toe. Their big brother, Joe, has given up his room for Mother and Father and is sleeping downstairs with Grandfather. In a few days time we move in to our new home.

Our new home! I can scarcely believe it. I look at the stars and tell myself that when we get up in the morning the sky will still be clear of smoke. But it's so hard to believe. In Manchester, the sky is never entirely dark at night, and by day a thick pall of smoke hides the sun even in midsummer. But now I'll be able to feel the sun on my face.

It was *such* a long journey. A whole day it's taken us to travel to Bank Top from Ancoats! I feel so stiff and sore from the jolting of that cart, but I'm too excited and restless for sleep. It's lucky I'll not have to rise early tomorrow. Father said I'll not be starting work until next week. A whole week I have to explore this wonderful place! To walk across fields and hills and breathe in air not tainted by smoke and soot.

Monday 13 March

Didn't know where I was this morning and when I heard the mill bell ring I nearly fell downstairs in panic, half-dressed. Mother laughed to see the expression on my face.

Peter and Joe Cooke and Father had already gone to the mill, but several young Cooke faces grinned up at me from the table and I was told to pull up a box. Freshly baked bread and oatcakes for breakfast. Delicious! Mrs Cooke baked both in her oven. Imagine that – their very own oven for baking! As soon as we'd finished, Mother got Mrs Cooke to show it to her. *And* there's a boiler for heating up the water. Mother was so full of envy, sighing and exclaiming, and she made Mrs Cooke show her again and again how they worked. There's also a slopstone for washing and scrubbing – and fresh water is piped into the house! No need to go out for it. Most extraordinary of all – gas is piped into the house from the mill! We've never heard of such a thing before. I felt as if I must be standing in the master's house. I told Mrs Cooke so and she laughed and told me that the masters live in very grand houses indeed.

And the Cooke's cottage even has its own privy! Mrs Cooke said that all the Ashworth cottages have their own privies.

After we'd finished our tour, Mother shooed us all outside into the garden. I'd been longing to see it. I hadn't properly – only in the dark and from the window. It's quite small, bounded by a fence and iron gates. Grandfather and I walked slowly round it while Emmy ran down the street with Harriet and Jenny. The winter snow has gone now and I can see that the soil here is thick and solid as clay.

Beyond the garden there are fields and woods and then the hilly moors rise up beyond. I sat on the grass and just stared and stared at it all. I could not believe where I was.

Tuesday 14 March

Jenny and Harriet took Emmy with them to school today. Oh, it was hard watching them go. Every word Peter Cooke has said about the school has made me so aware of what I'm missing. All the children here stay at school until they're nine and then those who start at the mill still spend part of their day there until they're thirteen. It's far better than most factory schools, Peter Cooke says. But I'll be working full time. I have no choice but to make do with the library.

Peter Cooke came up to me later. "Your father has told me that you are a fine scholar," he said. He told me that there's an excellent library and reading room in the village and that Mr Ashworth encourages his hands to study. "Maybe one day you too will become a teacher," he said. But I'll not let myself think about that now. Tomorrow we move into our new house and I'm looking forward to it!

Wednesday 15 March

Our new home lies just to the west of Bank Top. It stands on rising ground in a small row of cottages, about a mile's walk from the village. It looks quite old but it's solidly built of stone like all the cottages here. Peter Cooke helped us move. He's a big man, even bigger than Father, and does not look like a spinner at all. I asked him what he plans to do in America and he said that he wants to buy a little piece of land in the West and build a house on it. Land is still cheap there, he says, and he has savings. His words made me smile. He looks just like a farmer.

The cottage is so small after the Cookes'. There are two rooms downstairs – one a little scullery off the living room. No kitchen. No piped water or gas. No oven. We must fetch water from the well, about a ten-minute walk from the cottage. Upstairs there are two more rooms. The walls have been whitewashed but could do with a new coat. Mother nodded her head as we went from one room to the next. She was so quiet that I couldn't tell what she was thinking but though it's not as well fitted out as the Cookes', it's better than I'd expected. Our garden is quite small and very overgrown, and at the end is a stone wall. Beyond we look west to the moors and hills. As I stood outside with Grandfather, I shut my eyes and tried to imagine how it will look in the summer. For a time I forgot the school, I even forgot I'd soon be returning to work. It may sound odd but as I stood there, the chill March wind blowing on my face, I felt as if I'd stepped into the country of Grandfather's childhood at last.

Mother called us in and we cleared out the fireplace and lit the fire. We have a plentiful supply of coal and there is kindling to be found nearby. The Cookes stayed to help us clean, for the cottage is quite dirty. And it's quite a lug from the well with the water!

When Father came home he glanced quickly at Mother to see what she thought. Very anxious his face looked. "Well, there's no kitchen, no oven, there's a walk for the water, and it's a bit small," she said. Then she smiled a slow smile. "But there's no house at the back of it, and it has its own garden. I like it." Such relief on Father's face!

Sunday 19 March

The Cookes left early today, and we were sad to see them go, for though we've known them just a week we've become very fond of them. They told us that they'll write, but our faces were downcast as we helped them pack up the wagon for the first stage of their journey to America. Last night I'd written a letter to Jack and Mr Cooke has promised to give it to him. Tomorrow I begin work. That old feeling of dread swept over me again and I went early to bed.

Monday 20 March

Up at 4.30. It was so cold and dark that I fumbled with frozen fingers trying to pull on my clothes. How I envied Emmy, still fast asleep in bed. The days are growing longer now but it's a long walk to work and very cold; my hands and feet were red and almost numb with it by the time I reached the mill. As we walked in to the mill yard I saw plain stone walls rear up ahead of me. I tried not to look at them but already I fancied I could hear the shrieking of the engine, the clattering of hundreds of mules and looms that you can still hear even in the carding room.

After we'd broken for breakfast, tubs of steaming hot water – soap and towels too – were carried in and laid out for washing. It's already clear that this will be a better place to work. There's a list of rules pinned to the wall, and the fines are just as heavy as before, but no one here seems to have trouble reading them. The rooms are well ventilated by fans – even the privies! And no bother with fluff in the drinking water. It was changed for fresh several times. How good it is to be able to drink water that is not full of fluff, and breathe in air that doesn't make you choke.

It's too long a walk to go home for dinner so I bought a pie in the cookshop and ate it in the yard, my shawl wrapped tightly round me. Then Bridget – the woman I work with – showed me the gardens laid out near the mill where the Ashworths grow their fruit and vegetables. There are even little houses made out of glass where fruits are tended – peaches and grapes

Bridget told me in answer to my questions. They need the warmth to grow, she said when I asked her about the glasshouses. I told her I thought the gardens were beautiful and how I'd much rather work in them than in the mill. She laughed but I saw how curiously she looked at me.

The carding room hands are not sure what to make of me, I think. They've heard that I'm a Manchester girl and some of them seem wary of me. But I am a country girl at heart and one day they'll learn that too.

Wednesday 29 March

Awoke this morning to find that snow has fallen in the night. It made me gasp. The garden looked thick with it but when we went out we found it was not so deep, though it was hard following the path to the mill. Arrived with frozen feet and fingers and the hem of my dress soaking wet. Everyone who was able turned out later to help clear the snow from the road that runs through the village to the mill. The wagons had been hard put to reach the mill with the raw cotton this morning and this evening they must make the long journey back again with the finished cloth.

In Manchester the snow soon turns a dirty brown. But here the fields stay so white and clean. I worried about the garden but Grandfather says that the snow will protect the plants from frost. "A nice little blanket it makes for them," he said. Country life is still so strange to me and there's much I need to learn.

Sunday 2 April

We went to chapel today. Our whole family together! I thought Mother would put up a fuss when Father told her that he expected her to accompany him, but she agreed meekly enough, even though she's always made it clear just what she thinks about chapel-goers. Thought I'd fall through the floor!

Saturday 8 April

Snow has melted at last but the water in the bucket was still frozen when I came downstairs this morning. But little green shoots are beginning to show in the garden. I'm so excited to see these first small signs of spring. Soon we'll plant comfrey and marjoram and marigolds. And when the warm weather comes Grandfather's going to show me where to find wild herbs and plants to help soothe the ache in his hands.

The house was spotless when I got home! I'd thought I'd be pressed to help with the chores but Emmy told me *she'd* helped Mother that morning. She sounded very proud, and it's all done, even that awful rough-stoning! It doesn't take as long as it did in Ancoats, Mother said. There's no need to wipe down the walls and furniture each week. I was glad to hear that for I was itching to open the book I've borrowed from the library. It's called *Oliver Twist* and is a new novel by a man named Charles Dickens. The sad tale of the orphan boy had me in tears when I began it yesterday and I'm finding it so hard to put down.

That library is wonderful! There's all sorts there: the Bible and religious books of course but other books too, and journals. I was at quite a loss at first but then a lady came over to me and said her name was Mrs Dawes, and could she help. There was something about her that reminded me of Miss Croom, and before I knew where I was I found myself telling her all about school and how much I missed it. I felt a bit embarrassed when I'd done, but she smiled at me so kindly and asked so many questions about me and the sort of books I like to read. Feel determined now that I'm going to read seriously again – proper books, not those silly novelettes Sarah was so stuck on. Mrs Dawes has told me that she teaches at the school – and she wants to know what I think about the book when I bring it back! I felt so happy when I left that library – I didn't know where I was walking and it was quite dark by the time I got home.

As we sat round the table this evening, I found myself thinking of William. I feel sure he would have loved it here. We all love it, though Mother is a bit of a worry to us. She's so quiet and withdrawn sometimes. She's not yet met our neighbours and the days must seem long and lonely with just Grandfather for company.

Sunday 23 April

Bridget walked over for tea this afternoon. She and Mother got on ever so well – I can't remember when I've last seen Mother so talkative. I sat and listened while they swapped stories about Bolton and Manchester. And Mother had much to tell her – for Bridget has never been to Manchester. Never! Nor even left Bolton until she came to work here. Her eyes opened wide with horror when Mother told her about the riots.

"The strikers came here," Bridget said. "But they were peaceful enough – poor people – they were so hungry that they went up to Mr Ashworth's home and begged for bread. Most respectful though, I'm told they were. Not a single piece of fruit in Mr Ashworth's garden did they touch! The mill had to be shut all the same, mind, but we returned to work after a week. We none of us wanted to strike."

Mother told her how much she wished we'd been able to live in the village. "I miss the town in some ways," she said. "It is so quiet here. We'd hoped to be able to rent the Cookes' cottage when they emigrated but it was already promised to someone else."

Tuesday 25 April

Sometimes now when we get home from the mill, Mother's waiting on the step. All smiles when she sees us. It's as if last year's been blotted out. And Mother and Father never seem to argue either – not like they did in Manchester, and never a word is said about the Chartists. I don't think Father bothers to read the *Northern Star* for all there's a copy in the library. I saw it yesterday when I went back to borrow a new book. It gave me such a funny feeling to see it lying there. I picked it up but as I began to read suddenly it all came back – the fights between Mother and Father, the strike – and that horrible Bob Wavenshawe. Put it down quickly – didn't want to think about that time.

Saturday 29 April

Mr Ashworth has spoken to Father – about *me*! Father said he'd heard from Mr Harris, the overlooker, that I'm interested in reading and that I'm studious and hardworking. Father told Mr Ashworth that I did well at school and was commended by my teacher. Mr Ashworth sounded most interested, said Father. He's going to speak to Mrs Dawes about me. I could scarcely catch my breath when I heard that! I remember what Miss Croom said to me when I left Manchester. "When your chance comes, seize it." Has it come now? Diary, will it ever come? Or will I always be a mill girl? I do not know the answer, but I feel more content now. I do not know what has caused this change in me. I don't think it's just Mr Ashworth's words. Or even the help I've had from Mrs Dawes. Is it living in the country that has helped me to see things in a new light? Or is it that I'm beginning to grow up at last? Maybe I *will* become a teacher one day. Perhaps dreams do sometimes come true after all…

My diary has brought me so much comfort. And

now it is nearly finished. There's just a little space left for me to write on now. And that is just as well because I must stop and write to Jack – while there's still enough light to do so.

Historical Note

In the early Eighteenth Century there was no industry in Britain as we know it today. Most people worked in the country on the land, and spinning and weaving were done at home. There were few machines and these were not very fast or efficient. But as the century drew on, all this began to change. The population grew rapidly, increasing the need for food, cheap cloth, and other goods. Better farming methods and faster machines began to be developed to meet this need. The great changes to people's lives these brought about led to this period being known as "The Industrial Revolution".

One of the most important goods produced in Britain was cotton cloth. Cheap cotton imported from abroad had already replaced wool as the main textile in Britain, but in the early Eighteenth Century it could only be turned into cloth very slowly under the old methods of producing it at home. But with the invention of John Kay's Flying Shuttle the process of weaving cotton and woollen cloth began to be speeded up. Then, in 1764, James Hargreaves invented the

Spinning Jenny. This new spinning machine allowed one worker to spin as much as eight people had done on a traditional spinning wheel. As the century drew on, other inventions such as Arkwright's Water Frame, Crompton's Spinning Mule and Cartwright's Power Loom led to spinning and weaving beginning to be transferred from the home to factories – known as mills.

Most of these new cotton mills were built in the north. Here they had easy access to water and coal, which they needed to work. And, most importantly, the damp climate of the north helped stop the cotton threads from breaking too easily.

Power for the early mills was provided by water wheels. But with James Watt's improvements to Newcomen's Steam Engine, industry was transformed. Steam-power took over from water-power. These new steam engines were capable of powering many more machines, but they needed a lot of coal to make them run. This meant mills either needed to be near the coal-fields, or there had to be a more efficient way of getting coal to the mills. The growth of canals and, later, railways made it much easier to transport both the coal and cotton goods from warehouse to factory and market. More mills sprang up, and towns began to grow up around them. But one more thing was needed – people.

The early country mills often found it hard to get labour, and had relied on "apprentices" to operate the machines. These were often children, brought in from other parts of Britain where there was no work for them or their families. They weren't apprentices in the usual sense – merely a source of cheap labour, and often they were treated very badly. It was not until 1802 that the first of a number of Factory Acts attempted to change their plight by limiting the number of hours they were allowed to work to twelve.

But as the century drew on, more country people were forced to turn to the mills for work. Working and living conditions in the rapidly growing factory towns were very bad. Cheap houses had to be built hurriedly for the hundreds of workers that flocked to the towns in search of work, and many people were forced to live squashed together in tiny houses – sometimes several families to a room, or even in a cellar. It was difficult to keep the houses clean, cooking facilities were very limited if they existed at all, and often one street or "court" had to share one toilet. Water came from a pump or tap in the street, or even straight out of the canals. Rubbish was thrown into the street and hardly ever collected. Countless factories belched out sooty smoke all day long so that the air was very polluted. Not surprisingly, disease was rife.

And few of the masters of the factories and workshops cared anything about the long hours worked by their "hands" and the low wages they were paid.

But many people did not want to work in the factories, and continued to work at home – mainly the handloom weavers, who continued to supply the mills with woven cloth until well into the Nineteenth Century. However, as more efficient power looms began to be introduced into the mills, the handloom weavers couldn't produce cloth fast enough and were forced either to seek alternative employment or put up with very low rates for their work. And there were fewer jobs for male handloom weavers to turn to in the cotton industry. By this time most of the labour was being carried out by women and children – they could be paid less, and anyway, with the exception of the hand-operated spinning "mules", the machines didn't require much physical strength to operate.

As the Nineteenth Century progressed, further changes to the machines meant that fewer workers were needed to operate them. All this led to further unemployment and hunger.

But many workers were determined to change things. Back in the 1730s, convinced that the new machines would take away their means of earning a living, a mob had broken into John Kay's house and smashed everything they could find. John Kay himself had been forced to flee to France. Then, in the early years of the Nineteenth Century, workers had roamed the countryside, setting fire to the factories and smashing machines. These men were called "Luddites", after Ned Lud, a (probably imaginary) man who was supposed to be their leader. Riots and other disturbances followed – such as in 1811 in London at Spa Fields, and then in 1819 when mill workers gathered in St Peter's Fields in Manchester to listen to the words of an orator called Henry Hunt. The local magistrates were so alarmed that they sent in the Yeomanry and regular soldiers to arrest Hunt. In the stampede that followed, eleven people were killed and hundreds more injured. For many years afterwards the "Peterloo Massacre", as it became known, was remembered in Manchester by an annual procession of Chartists through the town. The white hat worn by Hunt and green ribbons were adopted as Chartist colours.

Chartism grew out of early radical movements like these. The Chartists believed that giving working men the vote would automatically lead to improvements in their lives and working conditions. At that time, few people were allowed to vote and ordinary people could not stand for Parliament. The Reform Act, which had been passed in 1832, had given the vote to more people than before, but ordinary working men (and all women) were still unable to have any say in who ran the country.

The Chartists were named after the People's Charter, which was drawn up by two of the movement's founders, William Lovett, a cabinet maker, and Francis Place, a master tailor. The main points of the Charter (the famous "Six Points") were:

The vote for all men over 21.

Annual General Elections.

Voting by secret ballots at elections.

Abolition of the requirement for MPs to be property owners.

Payment of MPs.

More equal electoral districts.

The Chartists made three attempts to get Parliament to adopt the Charter.

The first "Petition", presented to Parliament in 1839, was three miles long and bore one million signatures. But it was rejected by Parliament and uprisings followed. The principal leaders were imprisoned and the movement faltered. But one of the Chartist leaders, an Irish landowner called Fergus O'Connor, attempted to revitalize the movement. He did this partly through the Chartist paper – *The Northern Star* – which he himself set up in 1838. And on his release from prison he formed the National Charter Association (NCA) by drawing together local Chartist groups and working men's associations. Members were given a card bearing the words: "This is our Charter, God is our guide."

O'Connor was an inspiring and charismatic leader and an excellent speaker, but his willingness to advocate physical force where peaceful methods of achieving his aims failed, upset more moderate leaders like Lovett and Place.

On 2 May 1842, the Petition was again presented to Parliament. This time it was signed by three million men and women, but again it was turned down by Parliament, and in August strikes broke out. For some years the cotton industry had been in crisis as the demand for cotton had fallen. Poor harvests made matters still worse by pushing up the cost of food. (This time became known as the "Hungry Forties".) Many workers were forced to work "short time" or lose their jobs. Some trades had unions, but unions in those days lacked the powers they have now, and with so many thrown out of work there was little unions could do to help their members. Not only cotton workers, but other workers such as miners, shopkeepers, pawnbrokers, craftsmen and labourers were affected. Towns like Manchester had also attracted large numbers of Irish who came to the town looking for work, and left even worse conditions at home.

Under the old system of poor relief, the unemployed could have expected some help from their parish. But the New Poor Law, introduced in England in 1834, meant that there was little provision for the unemployed beyond going to the workhouse – or returning home to still worse privation. Many joined the Chartist movement. Others – mainly manufacturers, bankers and businessmen – supported the Anti Corn Law League (ACLL).

The Corn Laws had kept the price of grain and cost of food artificially high since the end of the Napoleonic Wars, and this in turn depressed the demand for manufactured goods since people had to spend more of their earnings on food. The ACLL wanted the Corn Laws repealed. By doing so, they argued, they would be able to reduce their costs and sell more goods both at home in Britain and abroad.

Manchester and the surrounding manufacturing towns became a hub of political activity. Throughout the summer of 1842, mass-meetings were held by different movements. Then, in August, some of the cotton masters decided to reduce wages. The strike and riots that then broke out in the manufacturing districts were to become known as the "Plug Plot" riots, as the striking mill workers pulled plugs from the boilers to stop steam engines from supplying power to the machines. The strike spread rapidly from the mills to the coal-fields and to other parts of industry as well, leading the government to fear that there was indeed a Chartist plot behind the strike. In fact, there is much controversy over the part the Chartists played in organizing the strike. Many Chartist meetings were held in towns like Manchester during the strike, but hunger and distress at last forced the workers to abandon their demands and return to work.

In 1848 – a time of revolutions and uprisings in Europe – there was a last burst of Chartist activity. A rally at Kennington Common was held and the Charter again presented to Parliament. It was claimed that six million people signed the Petition, but on close investigation many of the signatures were discovered to be false (Queen Victoria, "Flat Nose" and "Pug Face" were names found amongst them!) and the Petition was rejected for a third time. After this, the movement gradually petered out. But though Chartism as a movement failed, all but one of the "Six points" (annual elections) eventually became law. During the Nineteenth Century too, unions slowly became more powerful, strikes were legalized and factory reforms gradually improved conditions in the mills, factories and mines. But it was to be a very long time before the lives of the cotton workers really improved.

Timeline

1733 John Kay's Flying Shuttle is invented.

1764 James Hargreaves' Spinning Jenny.

1769 Richard Arkwright's Water Frame.

James Watt's improved steam engine.

1779 Samuel Crompton's spinning mule.

1785 Edmund Cartwright's power loom.

1789 The first steam-powered cotton mill is built.

1802 First Factory Act. It sets a maximum twelve-hour day for apprentices in factories.

1819 A further Factory Act limits the working hours of children under sixteen to twelve hours a day (in textile mills).

The "Peterloo" Massacre in Manchester.

1833 Another Factory Act. Under this act, no one under nine can be employed in a textile mill. Nine to thirteen year olds can work up to nine hours a day, with two hours' schooling and thirteen–eighteen year olds up to twelve hours a day. Factory inspectors are appointed to check that the provisions of the Act are carried out.

1837 Victoria becomes Queen.

1839 The first Chartist Petition is presented to Parliament, but is rejected.

1842 The second Chartist Petition is presented to Parliament. Again it is rejected and riots – the so-called "Plug Plot" riots – break out in industrial Britain.

1844 Ragged schools for children of the poor are set up.

1846 Sir James Kay-Shuttleworth's system of pupil-teachers is introduced. Under this plan, bright pupils of thirteen are appointed to assist teachers. At eighteen they go on to train as teachers at college.

Sir Robert Peel repeals the "Corn Laws".

1847 The "Ten Hour" Factory Act becomes law. Children under eighteen and women employed in textile mills can work no more than ten hours a day and up to 58 hours a week. However, many employers found a way round this by employing their workers in relay.

1848 A third attempt to get Parliament to ratify the Chartist Petition fails. Chartism as a movement begins to disintegrate soon afterwards.

1874 Disraeli's Factory Act establishes a ten-hour day for all workers.

1891 Elementary education becomes free for all children.

1918 All men over 21 get the vote.

1928 All women over 21 can now vote.

This cartoon shows mill workers being fed into a mincer and coming out as cotton clothes. The artist, George Cruikshank, wanted to show how the mill workers' jobs were so dangerous and unhealthy that it was costing them their lives to make the mill owners so rich.

Victoria Street Market, Manchester.

A carding room. Carding machines turned cotton wool into "slivers" (like thick rope). The slivers were collected in large cans.

A mule spinning room. These machines spun the cotton "slivers" into cotton thread. A child is shown sweeping up waste cotton and dirt from in and under the machines. It was a dangerous job — one slip and the ever-moving machinery might hit you.

A Manchester slum dwelling in the Nineteenth Century. The child in the corner is lying on a pile of straw.

A cotton mill on Great Ancoats Street, Manchester.

Fergus O'Connor, one of the Chartist leaders.

The Chartist's Great Petition of 1842 being taken to London to be presented to Parliament.

RULES
TO BE OBSERVED
By the Hands Employed in
THIS MILL.

RULE 1. All the Overlookers shall be on the premises first and last.

2. Any Person coming too late shall be fined as follows:—for 5 minutes 2d, 10 minutes 4d, and 15 minutes 6d, &c.

3. For any Bobbins found on the floor 1d for each Bobbin.

4. For single Drawing, Slubbing, or Roving 2d for each single end.

5. For Waste on the floor 2d.

6. For any Oil wasted or spilled on the floor 2d each offence, besides paying for the value of the Oil.

7. For any broken Bobbins, they shall be paid for according to their value, and if there is any difficulty in ascertaining the guilty party, the same shall be paid for by the whole using such Bobbins.

8. Any person neglecting to Oil at the proper times shall be fined 2d.

9. Any person leaving their Work and found Talking with any of the other workpeople shall be fined 2d for each offence.

10. For every Oath or insolent language, 3d for the first offence, and if repeated they shall be dismissed.

11. The Machinery shall be swept and cleaned down every meal time.

12. All persons in our employ shall serve Four Weeks' Notice before leaving their employ; but L. WHITAKER & SONS, shall and will turn any person off without notice being given.

13. If two persons are known to be in one Necessary together they shall be fined 3d each; and if any Man or Boy go into the Women's Necessary he shall be instantly dismissed.

14. Any person wilfully or negligently breaking the Machinery, damaging the Brushes, making too much Waste, &c., they shall pay for the same to its full value.

15. Any person hanging anything on the Gas Pendants will be fined 2d.

16. The Masters would recommend that all their workpeople Wash themselves every morning, but they shall Wash themselves at least twice every week, Monday Morning and Thursday morning; and any found not washed will be fined 3d for each offence.

17. The Grinders, Drawers, Slubbers and Rovers shall sweep at least eight times in the day as follows, in the Morning at 7½, 9½, 11 and 12; and in the Afternoon at 1½, 2½, 3½, 4½ and 5½ o'clock; and to notice the Board hung up, when the black side is turned that is the time to sweep, and only quarter of an hour will be allowed for sweeping. The Spinners shall sweep as follows, in the Morning at 7½, 10 and 12; in the Afternoon at 3 and 5½ o'clock. Any neglecting to sweep at the time will be fined 2d for each offence.

18. Any persons found Smoking on the premises will be instantly dismissed.

19. Any person found away from their usual place of work, except for necessary purposes, or Talking with any one out of their own Alley will be fined 2d for each offence.

20. Any person bringing dirty Bobbins will be fined 1d for each Bobbin.

21. Any person wilfully damaging this Notice will be dismissed.

The Overlookers are strictly enjoined to attend to these Rules, and they will be responsible to the Masters for the Workpeople observing them.

WATER-FOOT MILL, NEAR HASLINGDEN.
SEPTEMBER, 1851.

J. Read, Printer, and Bookbinder, Haslingden.

Mill rules and fines. The mills all had strict rules for the workers. They were displayed in the mill on posters like this, and if workers broke any of the rules they could be fined or even dismissed.

TO THE FUSTIAN JACKETS, BLISTERED HANDS, AND UNSHORN CHINS

MY BELOVED FRIENDS,

On the 11th of May I was snatched from you by the ruthless arm of tyranny; on Monday next I shall be restored to you by the hand of Providence, and upon that day you shall judge for yourselves whether nearly sixteen months of solitary-mind, solitary-confinement in a condemned cell, in a felon's prison, and treated brutally and in violation of every rule by which prison discipline is administered to the worst of felons, has damped my ardour, or slackened my zeal. On Monday you shall judge whether oppression has broken O'Connor's heart, or O'Connor has broken oppression's head. Till then, farewell. *On leaving you, my motto was Universal Suffrage and no Surrender.* On joining you once more, the same words shall be upon my banner. O! Monday will be a great and glorious day for Chartism and right. I shall, with God's help, aided by the people's prayers, gain a giant's strength, 'twixt this and the hour for which I pant.

Ever your fond and devoted friend,

To the death,

FEARGUS O'CONNOR.

York Castle, 25th of 16th month of confinement
in the Condemned Cell.

Fergus O'Connor's letter written to the Chartists from prison. It was published in the Northern Star *newspaper.*

Picture acknowledgments

P 214	Tremendous Sacrifice!, George Cruikshank, Bettmann/Hulton
P 215 (top)	Victoria Street Market, Manchester Central Library, Local Studies Unit
P 215 (bottom)	Carding, Manchester Central Library, Local Studies Unit
P 216	Mule Spinning, Manchester Central Library, Local Studies Unit
P 217 (top)	Manchester Slum Scene, *Illustrated London News*, Mary Evans Picture Library
P 217 (bottom)	Mr Pollards Cotton Twist Mill, Ancoats, Manchester Central Library, Local Studies Unit
P 218 (top)	Fergus O'Connor, Mary Evans Picture Library
P 218 (bottom)	Great Petition of 1842, By permission of People's History Museum
P 219	Mill Rules, By permission of People's History Museum
P 220	Fergus O'Connor's letter to the *Northern Star*, By permission of People's History Museum

A number of people and organizations have helped me with my research for this book. In particular I'd like to thank the following: Cecil Black, Duncan Broady (Greater Manchester Police Museum), Frances Casey (National Army Museum), Adam Daber and staff at Quarry Bank Mill (National Trust), Styal, Kate Dickson and Steve Little (Ancoats Building Preservation Trust), Ian Gibson and the staff of Helmshore Textile Museums, Lancashire, Manchester Central Library Local Studies Unit, Merseyside Maritime Museum, Liverpool, Andy Pearce (People's History Museum, Manchester), Professor M E Rose (Manchester University), Ray Walker (Working Class Movement Library, Salford), Pauline Webb (Museum of Science and Industry, Manchester).

My thanks also go to Jill Sawyer at Scholastic and to Ali Evans for editing the book.

The Hunger
The Diary of Phyllis McCormack
Ireland 1845-1847

Voyage on the Great Titanic
The Diary of Margaret Anne Brady
1912

Blitz
The Diary of Edie Benson
London 1940-1941

The Crystal Palace
The Diary of Lily Hicks
London 1850-1851

Twentieth-Century Girl
The Diary of Flora Bonnington
London 1899-1900

My Story.

My Tudor Queen
The Diary of Eva De Puebla
London 1501-1513

The '45 Rising
The Diary of Euphemia Grant
Scotland 1745-1746

The Great Plague
The Diary of Alice Paynton
London 1665-1666

Transported
The Diary of Elizabeth Harvey
Australia 1790

Featuring young men at the centre of each story, this brand-new series covers significant conflicts in world history.

Civil War
Thomas Adamson
England 1643-1650

Trafalgar
James Grant
HMS Norseman 1799-1806

The Trenches
Billy Stevens
The Western Front 1914-1918

Battle of Britain
Harry Woods
England 1939-1941